The Star outside My WINDOW

Also by Onjali Q. Raúf

The Boy at the Back of the Class
The Night Bus Hero

The Star outside my Window

Onjali Q. Raúf

DELACORTE PRESS

Text copyright © 2019 by Onjali Q. Raúf
Jacket art copyright © 2019, 2020 by Pippa Curnick
Map illustrations copyright © 2019 by Pippa Curnick

All rights reserved. Published in the United States by Delacorte Press, an imprint of Random House Children's Books, a division of Penguin Random House LLC, New York. Originally published in paperback by Orion Children's Books, an imprint of Hachette Children's Group of Hodder and Stoughton, Hachette UK, London, in 2019.

Delacorte Press is a registered trademark and the colophon is a trademark of Penguin Random House LLC.

Visit us on the Web! rhcbooks.com

Educators and librarians, for a variety of teaching tools, visit us at RHTeachersLibrarians.com

Library of Congress Cataloging-in-Publication Data
Names: Raúf, Onjali Q., author.
Title: The star outside my window / Onjali Q. Raúf.
Description: First U.S. edition. | New York : Delacorte Press, [2021] |
Originally published in paperback by Orion Children's Books, Hachette UK, London, in 2019. | Audience: Ages 8–12. | Summary: Ten-year-old Aniyah and her little brother Noah find themselves living in foster care after the sudden disappearance of their mom, but with her life in disarray, Aniyah knows just one thing for sure—her mom is not gone forever.
Identifiers: LCCN 2020040488 (print) | LCCN 2020040489 (ebook) |
ISBN 978-0-593-30227-9 (hardback) | ISBN 978-0-593-30228-6 (library binding) |
ISBN 978-0-593-30229-3 (ebook)
Subjects: CYAC: Foster children—Fiction. | Foster home care—Fiction. |
Brothers and sisters—Fiction. | Family violence—Fiction.
Classification: LCC PZ7.1.R378 St 2021 (print) | LCC PZ7.1.R378 (ebook) |
DDC [Fic]—dc23

The text of this book is set in 11.8-point Simoncini Garamond.
Interior design by Cathy Bobak
Interior firework art and some interior constellation art used under license from Shutterstock.com

Printed in the United States of America
10 9 8 7 6 5 4 3 2 1
First U.S. Edition

For my aunt, Mumtahina (Ruma) Jannat,
whose star sits beside the moon.
For the two rays of light she was forced to leave behind,
and all children surviving the impacts of domestic* abuse.
And for my mum and Zak. Always.

---

* The author of this story does not like to link the word "domestic" to the word "abuse." This is because the word "domestic" implies that abuses happening inside the home should remain private, even when they constitute a crime, while also making many people too embarrassed to report abuses. However, as the prevailing term, she has used it throughout this book for clarity.

Буди скроман, јер си створен од земље.
Буди племенит, јер си направљен од звезда.

Be humble, because you are made of the earth.
Be noble, because you are made of stars.

—Serbian Proverb (attributed)

Determined like an asteroid burning, flaming
through the skies.

—Hugo Rees (ten years old, poet, Cranmore Prep)

CONTENTS

Before We Take Flight . . .

This is a story written for everyone.

But it's also a story that may cause distress or upset for anyone who is seeing or experiencing abuse in their own home, and is having to be extra-especially brave and strong.

If you should happen to be one such special person, or are worried that someone you know is being hurt, please turn to the back of this book to learn more about people who are ready and waiting to help you and your loved ones. No matter how big or small you—or your loved ones—may be.

Sending you all our love and stardust . . .

BICYCLE ROUTE MAP

Waverley Village
to
Greenwich

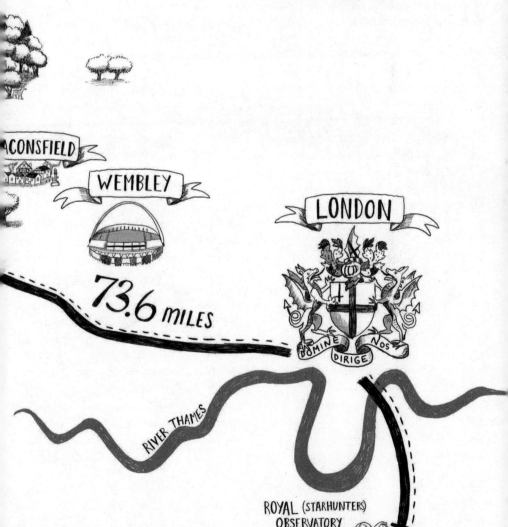

CONSFIELD

WEMBLEY

LONDON

73.6 MILES

DOMINE NOS
DIRIGE

RIVER THAMES

ROYAL (STARHUNTERS)
OBSERVATORY
GREENWICH

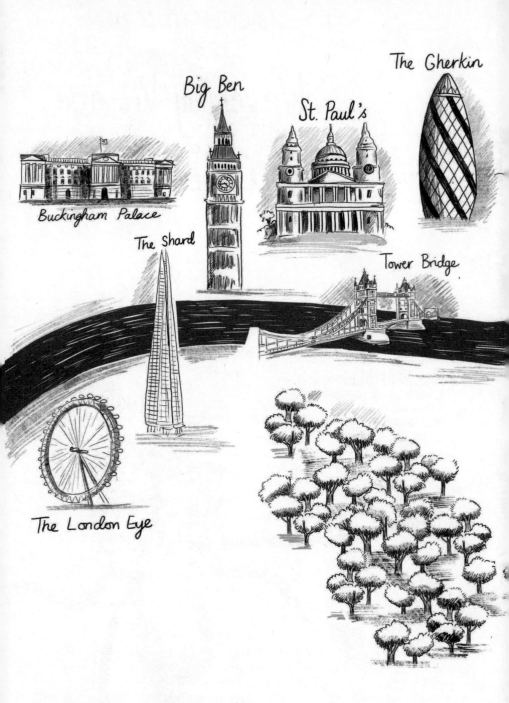

The Gherkin

Big Ben

St. Paul's

Buckingham Palace

The Shard

Tower Bridge

The London Eye

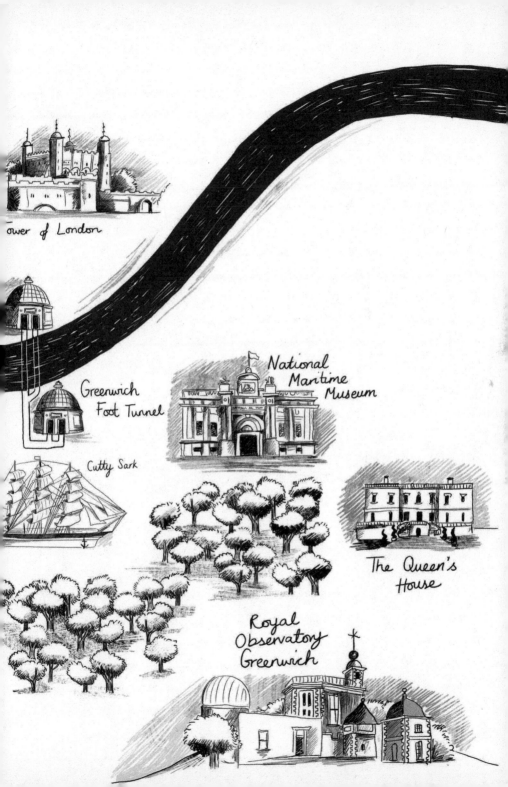

Tower of London

Greenwich
Foot Tunnel

National
Maritime
Museum

Cutty Sark

The Queen's
House

Royal
Observatory
Greenwich

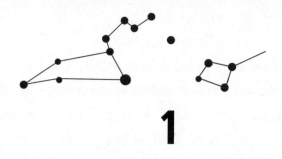

1

A Map to the Stars

I've always wanted to be a star hunter.

Everyone else calls them astronomers, but I think "star hunter" sounds much better, so that's what I'm going to call myself. But I'm not going to be the kind of star hunter that looks for old stars. I want to find the brand-new ones—the ones that have only just been born and are searching for the people they've left behind. I read in a library book once that stars can burn for millions and billions and even trillions of years. I hope that's true, because there's one star I don't ever want to stop burning. I don't know where it is yet, but I know it's out there, waiting for me to find it.

Back in my real house, where I lived with Mum and Dad, I had three whole shelves of books in my bedroom, and at least half of them were all about stars and space travel. The walls and ceiling were covered with posters and glow-in-the-dark stars that I'd begged Mum and Dad to get me. But the best thing in my room was my special star globe, which sat right next to my bed. From far away, it looked like a globe of the world—but it wasn't. It was a globe of the night sky, and instead of countries and oceans, it lit up with all the constellations you could ever think of. There was a different constellation every time you switched it on, and I knew all of them by heart. That's why new stars will be easy for me to spot when I'm a star hunter—if you know a picture by heart, it's easy to tell when something about it is different.

I wish Mum hadn't forgotten to pack the star globe. Sometimes I miss it so much that I wonder if I'll ever stop missing it. I miss it even more now that Noah and me have had to move to the strange new place we're living in right now.

We've been here for two days, and even though the house is much nicer than the last one we had to hide in with Mum, I'm not sure I like it here. It's full of creepy noises. Like floorboards creaking when there's no one there, invisible things tapping on the window at night as if they're trying to get in, and tiny squeaks and scratchings coming from behind the walls. My little brother, Noah, thinks the house is haunted—he gets so scared at bedtime that I have to make him lie down with his head under the covers and I hug him tight until he falls asleep. Noah's only five. It's OK for a five-year-old to be scared of ghosts, but it's silly for a ten-year-old to believe in them, so I won't. No matter how much the noises make me want to hide under the covers with him.

But it's not just the noises that make this house feel strange. It's the people in it too.

There's a boy called Travis who doesn't speak. He's eleven, tall and skinny, and looks like an elastic band that's been stretched too far. His teeth stick out from under his lips because of the big silver braces on them—his mouth looks like a builder tried to squeeze lots of bits of metal scaffolding inside and didn't know when to stop. Most of the time he just stares at me with his huge gray-brown eyes that stick out like Ping-Pong balls. I don't like people staring at me. My cheeks turn bright red and it makes me feel like running away. But he keeps doing it, even when I stare back at him.

Then there's Ben, who has huge, fluffy black hair that looks like it's been put on his head by a giant ice cream scoop. He's ten years old like me, with bright brown eyes that look like they're asking you a million questions, and a shiny round pimple on his left cheek that he keeps poking when he thinks no one is looking. He always wears a Newcastle United hooded sweatshirt the wrong way around, and eats popcorn and crisps from inside the hood as if it's a bowl. Ben says strange things and asks me lots of questions—as if he's a detective on a TV show and I'm a criminal. Questions like "Hey! Why are you here?" and "Do you guys need to get adopted too?" and "Holy big fat goalie, Aniyah! Don't you like fish sticks? Can I have them instead, then?" I hate being asked questions almost as much as I hate being stared at—especially when I don't know the answers and my voice isn't working. So whenever he asks me anything, I just look at the floor and shrug.

Finally, there's Sophie. Sophie's thirteen, which makes her the oldest out of all of us, but she's still shorter than Travis. Sophie has long, straight, bright red hair and exactly twenty-seven brown freckles across her nose. I counted them as soon as I met her, because I like freckles. I think freckles and stars look nearly the same—all tiny and fiery—and it's fun to see what shapes you can make out of them. I wish I had freckles, but I don't. Not even a single one. If Sophie and me were friends, I'd tell her that her freckles make the shape of a blue whale or a ship with three sails, depending on which way you connect them. But Sophie doesn't like me or Noah, so I don't think I'm ever going to be able to tell her that. I know she doesn't like us, because whenever Mrs. Iwuchukwu isn't looking, she gives us lots of I-hate-you stares and narrows her eyes and grits her teeth. Getting one of those stares always makes my hands and feet go ice-cold.

Mrs. Iwuchukwu is the woman who owns the house we're all living in, and is one of the strangest grown-ups I've ever met. She wears lots and lots of necklaces and beads and bracelets, so whenever she moves, she makes clunking noises like marbles moving inside a bag. She also smiles so much that I think her cheeks must hurt all the time. I've never seen anyone smile as much as she does. Most of the time I have to look around to see what she's smiling at, because usually you need a reason to smile. But Mrs. Iwuchukwu doesn't seem to need one. When I first met her, I thought she was Ben's mum, because they have the same kind of hair, all big and bouncy, and the exact same color skin. She has shiny bright pink lips and wears lots of glitter around her dark brown eyes and her accent makes her sound as if she's half singing and half telling you off. I don't know if me and Noah like Mrs. Iwuchukwu yet. But we have to try, and we have to try to make her like us too, because she's the only one who can keep us together now that everyone else has disappeared. That's what a foster mum does—keeps kids like me and Noah together when their mums and dads have disappeared.

I never knew what a foster mum was until two nights ago. I had a real mum until then, so I guess I never needed to know. But when Mum left, two policemen and a tall woman in a black suit came and said we had to go to a foster home so we could meet our new foster mum. I didn't like the sound of a "foster" anything—they sound like pretend things, things that try to make you believe they're yours when they're not. Noah didn't like the sound of them either and began to cry and scream and hiccup straightaway.

Noah only ever hiccups or cries when he gets really scared. Mum said it was my lifelong job to look after him, so when he started crying and hiccuping in front of the policemen and the woman in the suit, I tried to tell him with my eyes not to be scared because I was there to protect him. But I don't think he saw my eye-words, because he cried and hiccuped the whole time we were sitting in the back of the police car and then all through the night too. I wish I could have said nice things to him with my real words instead of just invisible ones, but my voice vanished when I heard Mum leaving us, and it still hasn't come back yet. I think it will come back just as soon as I find out where Mum is for sure.

That's why I can't wait until I'm a grown-up to become a star hunter—I have to become one right away so I can find out which part of the sky Mum is in now. Every star in the sky has a name and a story, and extra-superspecial stars become part of a constellation and part of an even bigger story. I know, because Mum explained the truth about stars to me properly after we watched *The Lion King* together.

The Lion King is my most favorite cartoon film of all time. Mum let me and Noah watch it whenever Dad came home from work and needed to move furniture around the house. Mum would wink and lock the door and, pointing the remote control at the telly, say, "Let's drown out the world, shall we?" Sometimes Dad would bang on the door and call for her and she would have to leave us alone, but we didn't mind watching it on our own too. Noah loved Pumbaa and Timon the best and always giggled and danced whenever they came on.

But my most favorite bit is when Simba's dad tells him that all the great lion kings of the past are looking down from the stars above, and that because of them, he doesn't ever have to feel alone. When I heard Simba's dad say that the very first time, I asked Mum if it was only kings that could become stars. It didn't seem fair that queens couldn't become stars too, and what happened if you didn't know anyone who was a king or queen in the first place? Did you have to be left all alone? Mum had frowned and looked down at me with her chocolaty-brown eyes. Then, after thinking about my question for a bit, she said that of course queens became stars too. And not only that, ordinary people who had extra-bright hearts sometimes went on to become the biggest stars in the sky—even bigger than the stars of the kings and queens! So everyone was bound to know at least one of the stars looking down on them.

I'm glad she told me that. Because if she hadn't, I wouldn't ever have known what the noise meant, when I heard Mum leave us to go and turn into a star.

As soon as Noah falls asleep and his arms go floppy enough to let go of me, I'm going to make a map of all the stars I can see from our window. I'll work on it every night until I've found all the new stars in the sky. I've got to try to find the brightest, newest star there is, because that one will be Mum's. I'll know it's hers when I see it, because Mum had the biggest, brightest heart out of anyone I ever knew. And people with the biggest, brightest hearts never end up in the ground. They end up in the sky.

2

The Foster-House Rules

Even though it's our third day in the foster house, for the first few seconds after I wake up, I forget that Mum is gone and that Dad can't find us, and that I'm not in my room at home anymore. But then my eyes start to see things properly and my brain starts to remember everything, and I wish I hadn't woken up at all. I squeeze my eyes tight again and hold on to the silver locket around my neck. I love my locket—it's round and shiny with swirls all over it. Mum and Dad bought it for me for my seventh birthday and it's the only thing I have left that reminds me of both of them. That's why every morning, after I remember they're not with me anymore, I hold it and squeeze my eyes shut tight and then open them suddenly—to give my eyeballs a surprise. I saw someone on TV do that once to help themselves wake up from a bad dream. But it doesn't work for me, because the picture doesn't change, which means the bad dream isn't a dream at all.

But that's not the worst thing about waking up in a foster house. The worst thing is sharing a bed with Noah and waking up to find that my legs are all cold and sticky because he's wet himself again. I know he can't help it and that he only does it because he's scared, but it's still annoying. I could sleep in the upper bunk bed like I'm supposed to, but then Noah would be all alone. Instead, I try to sleep right on the edge of the bed so that I stay dry. But it never works. I think when my voice comes back I'm going to ask for an umbrella.

So far, Mrs. Iwuchukwu hasn't told Noah off for wetting the bed. Instead, she acts like it's the best thing in the world for anyone to do! Every morning, she comes into our room, says, "Rise and shine!" and sniffs the air like a rabbit. Then she comes to the bed and pulls back the covers and cries out, "Ah! There it is!" as if she's found something special she's been looking for instead of just a big pool of pee. Laughing and waving me and Noah off the bed, she then twirls the wet bedsheet around her arms like a giant ball of cotton candy and says, "Better out than in! First rule of the house—when you need to go, you go!"

Being allowed to wet the bed isn't the only strange rule in this house. Mrs. Iwuchukwu seems to have lots of rules that are completely different from the ones we had at home. When the woman in the black suit and the policemen brought us to Mrs. Iwuchukwu's house, they didn't say anything about the foster-house rules. All they kept saying was "Everything's going to be OK" and "You have nothing to worry about now." But there are lots of things I worry about. Like what if I never get to go back to school and see my two best friends, Eddie and Kwan, ever again? Or what do I do if Noah gets hungry in the middle of the night and wants to go down to the kitchen to get something from the biscuit jar like we used to at home? Or how big is Mrs. Iwuchukwu's switch and what do we need to do to make sure it never gets flipped over to the wrong side? The switch question is the most important, because I know everyone has a switch inside them and, if it gets flipped, it can make them get angry and hurt you. Especially grown-ups who work hard like Dad. The woman in the black suit had said Mrs. Iwuchukwu was going to be working very hard to look after us, so I think she'll probably have a switch as big as Dad's. That's why I need to know all her rules. That way I can make sure that me and Noah won't break them.

I've been listening extra hard to Mrs. Iwuchukwu and watching Ben and Travis and Sophie too. But it's tricky to learn what the rules of a place are when nobody tells you them straightaway. It's like walking into a new school and never being told what might get you a detention. That's why I like stars. Up in the sky, the rules don't ever change, so nobody needs to say anything. New stars might be born and really old stars that don't have anyone to look after anymore might fade away, but otherwise, all the stars stay exactly where they are for millions of years, and never, ever move. But people aren't like stars. They don't come with flashing dots that you can join up whenever you want to know exactly who they are. So as well as being a star hunter I have to be a clue hunter too, and look for clues about what Mrs. Iwuchukwu's rules are and where her switch might be. I'm learning new rules every day, and so far, I've learned:

Rule Number One: **We can wet ourselves whenever we want to, and nobody will shout at us or make us stand in a corner.**

In fact, Mrs. Iwuchukwu smiles so much when Noah's wet the bed that I think he's starting to think it might be OK for him to pee in other places too. Last night before she told us to come in for tea, he asked me if it was OK for him to lift his leg and go on a tree, just like dogs do in the park. I shook my head, but I could tell he was still thinking about it when we went to bed, because he kept seeing how high his leg could go and looking over at the wardrobe in our room.

Rule Number Two: **We can cry and scream however loud we want to and Mrs. Iwuchukwu won't ever tell us to "Stop it!" or "Grow up!" or "Stop acting like a big baby!"**

Ben calls Noah a "champion screamer," because he screams and cries nearly all the time. That includes in the shower when he doesn't want Mrs. Iwuchukwu to wash him because she's not Mum, and in the morning when she's trying to help him get out of his pajamas, and in the evening when she's trying to help him get into his pajamas, and all the other times in between. But Mrs. Iwuchukwu doesn't seem to mind his screaming—not even one bit. She just smiles and nods and says, "That's it—let the monsters out, Noah! Remember, you can cry as *much* as you want, and as *loud* as you want, and for as *long* as you want. Just so long as you don't make yourself sick!" At home, Mum and Dad would never have allowed him to cry and scream for so long, but now that he can do it whenever he wants, I think he's starting to get bored, because his cries are getting shorter and his screams aren't so loud and screamy anymore.

Rule Number Three: **You can make a mess when you're eating and no one will ever tell you off or slap your hand.**

Mrs. Iwuchukwu didn't say this rule out loud, but I noticed it at breakfast on our very first day here. At home,

Mum always had to help us eat our food and cut all the bits to make sure nothing fell on the table or the floor in case Dad's switch got flipped. And sometimes before school, when Dad had been working very hard at the bank and needed us to be extra quiet and clean so that he could sleep in peace, Mum would give us breakfast wrapped in paper towels and make us eat by the car.

But in the foster house, Ben drops crumbs everywhere when he eats, and spreads them across his face too, and never says sorry. And Travis is allowed to put chocolate spread on his toast all on his own without someone making sure it's even and neat and hasn't spilled over. And Sophie can put different cereals into her bowl and mix them up and pour in her own milk. And at teatime, everyone's allowed to take whatever they want straight onto their plates and even have as much ketchup as they want, and Mrs. Iwuchukwu never says anything! They're all things Noah and me were never allowed to do at home, so now Noah gets excited whenever Mrs. Iwuchukwu says it's time to eat. I'm not hungry enough yet to eat anything properly, but after I find out where Mum's star is and my tummy stops hurting me so much, I think I'm going to like this rule.

Rule Number Four: **Music can be played in the kitchen, and it makes grown-ups become even stranger than they already are.**

Whenever Mrs. Iwuchukwu is in the kitchen, she switches on a bright red radio that sits on the windowsill next to some potted plants, and plays lots of songs that don't have any words in them—only piano notes and violins and orchestra sounds. Then she closes her eyes and hums loudly and dances around the kitchen and the dinner table as if someone invisible is dancing with her. Sometimes she grabs Travis and Ben and makes them dance with her too.

The first time it happened, Noah got so scared that he wouldn't let go of my arm, because at home, everything always had to be quiet and peaceful so that Dad could think straight. I never saw Mum dance or hum. Not ever. But when Mrs. Iwuchukwu started doing it, Travis smiled and hummed along, Sophie rolled her eyes but grinned at the same time, and Ben leaned in and said, "Don't worry—she always does this!"

I wasn't expecting to learn any more rules on our third day, because after everyone else had gone to school, Mrs. Iwuchukwu had us do the same things we did the first two days we were there. First she let us sit and draw and color in the living room until lunchtime, when we were allowed to watch television for half an hour. Then she read us a story and let us go and play in the garden until everyone came home. Playing in the garden made me realize that Mrs. Iwuchukwu's messes-are-OK rule was true outside too—because when Noah fell down and got mud all over his trousers, she didn't tell him off. Instead she said, "What a lovely color that dirt is, don't you think, Noah? Look at all those different shades of brown!" That made Noah immediately stop crying and bend over to look at the stains properly, as if he'd never really thought about it before.

After we were told to come inside again and Noah had changed into some pajama bottoms, Mrs. Iwuchukwu clapped her hands and said, "Right, Aniyah! Noah! The third day is a charm, so what shall we have for dinner today? Veggie lasagna? Or fish fingers and chips? Or spaghetti?" She waited for us to answer as she waved at us to sit down at the kitchen table. She was wearing golden glitter around her eyes today, and it made her eyelids look like sand on a beach when the sun's shining on it.

Noah cried out, "Spaghetti! I want spaghetti!"

"We having spaghetti?" A voice floated down the corridor, followed a few seconds later by Ben's hair and face popping around the corner of the kitchen door. The front door slammed shut, and Travis and Sophie came running into the kitchen too. They all dumped their schoolbags on the floor—except for Sophie, who said, "Ugh! Mum! Just call me down when it's ready!" before disappearing upstairs to her room.

I frowned, wondering how Mrs. Iwuchukwu could be Sophie's mum when they looked so different.

"Travis—how does spaghetti sound?"

Travis nodded at Mrs. Iwuchukwu and then turned to stare at me without blinking.

"Aniyah?"

Noah loved spaghetti, so I nodded, even though I still wasn't hungry.

"Good—big bowls of lovely spaghetti it is! Ben—hands washed, and then can you get the mozzarella out, please . . . the one in the packet . . . and cut it into slices. . . . Make sure you drain it properly first. And, Travis, you can get me some basil leaves—I'll need about . . . twenty. Chop-chop!" And Mrs. Iwuchukwu headed to the windowsill, clicked on the radio, and instantly filled the air with music. "Ah! Chopin!" she shouted as she began to dance.

I wanted to help too, but because my voice wasn't working, I couldn't tell anyone that yet, so I sat and watched with Noah instead. It's funny watching people chop things and get things and wash things and pour things when there's music playing—it's like watching a movie that's real. It made Noah clap his hands and make his knife and fork dance in the air too.

When everything was ready, Mrs. Iwuchukwu called Sophie down. She was still in her school uniform, which made me wish me and Noah still had our uniforms too. I had wanted to bring them with us from the hotel-that-wasn't-really-a-hotel, but the lady in the black suit had told us to leave them behind. That was when I knew I might never see my friends or school ever again.

Ben came and put a plate of cheese in the middle of the table. I had never seen that type of cheese before—it looked like a small roll of spongy bread that had been cut into thick round slices, except it was the color of white chalk. I was sure cheese was meant to be yellow, not white, and I knew right away I wasn't ever going to eat it.

Ben sat down in his chair, and after quickly tapping the spot on his cheek as if making sure it was still there, he asked, "Are you going to eat today, Aniyah? How come you're not ever hungry? I'm always hungry! What's your favorite cheese? Mine's this one! Do you want some?" He pushed the plate toward me.

I shook my head and looked over at Sophie. She was sitting at the end of the table next to Noah, and was giving him another I-hate-you stare because he was banging his knife and a toy car on the table. Then Travis came and sat down and started staring at me without blinking at all.

"Ben, can you be quiet for a minute and let everyone eat, please," ordered Mrs. Iwuchukwu as she came and put two bowls of bright red, extra-slippery spaghetti in front of me and Noah. Noah went to stab his spaghetti with his fork, but I grabbed his hand and shook my head to tell him to wait until we were allowed.

"Yeah, *Ben*!" whispered Sophie as soon as Mrs. Iwuchukwu went back to the kitchen to get everyone else's bowls. "Can you shut up please and stop being so stupid and *annoying*!"

Ben nodded seriously, but after staying quiet for exactly three seconds, he whispered, "Aniyah! You should try this garlic bread! It's the best!" He pushed the long stick of bread toward me, but I didn't want it, so I shook my head and pushed it back to him.

"Go on!" said Ben. "You can't have spaghetti without garlic bread! That's sacred-religious!"

"Ugh! You're so stupid, Ben! The word is *sacrilegious*!" said Sophie, rolling her eyes as if she couldn't believe she had to be at the same table as him.

Ignoring her, Ben pushed the garlic bread back to me. Travis stared some more.

I wanted to tell Ben that my stomach hurt and my throat

was blocked and that I didn't want to eat anything because nothing looked or smelled the way Mum used to make it, but I couldn't, so I pushed the bread away again. But as I brought my arm back toward me, I accidentally pushed my spaghetti bowl with my elbow and it suddenly flew off the table, turned upside down in the air, and crashed straight onto the floor!

Crack! Thud! Squelch!

The bowl instantly smashed into two big pieces, making tomato-sauce-covered spaghetti strings splatter onto the legs of my chair and the bright blue wall behind me. The floor looked as if an animal had been run over on it and all its insides had squeezed out everywhere. . . .

I jumped up and stood beside my chair without breathing and waited to be shouted at, my whole body starting to shake as if it had been dipped in ice. I heard Sophie gasp and Ben say, "Cricketing crickets!" and I could see Travis staring at me funny. Noah started to hiccup because he was getting frightened for me, just like he used to do whenever one of us dropped or spilled anything at home.

"*Mu-um!* Look what Aniyah's done!" shouted Sophie, sitting up straight. "She just *threw* the bowl onto the floor!"

I looked at Sophie and then at Mrs. Iwuchukwu in the kitchen. I opened my mouth to say it was just an accident and that it wasn't on purpose. But no noise came out.

"Aniyah, did you *throw* the bowl?" asked Mrs. Iwu-chukwu quietly as she walked over to the table with a frown.

I shook my head again.

"I don't like being lied to, Aniyah," said Mrs. Iwu-chukwu, raising her eyebrows. "It's the golden rule in this house. No matter what happens and no matter how naughty you've been or how upset you are, nobody is *ever* allowed to lie to me. I'm going to ask you again. Did you throw the bowl on purpose?"

I shook my head again and tried to make the words come out too. But my voice was still too far away to get to me in time.

"Sh-she d-didn't do it on p-purpose," said Travis. "It—it was an a-a-ac-shi-dent."

"Yeah," said Ben, looking at Sophie nervously.

Sophie narrowed her eyes at Travis and Ben and then, shaking her head, said, "They're lying, Mum, 'cause they don't want her to get grounded! I *saw* her do it! You put her bowl on the table for her, she waited for you to go back to the kitchen, and then she picked it up and threw it on the floor."

Mrs. Iwuchukwu took a deep breath and, after a few seconds, quietly said, "Aniyah, go upstairs to your room, please."

Ben frowned even harder. Travis looked down at his bowl. Noah began to hiccup so loudly that he made the table shake. I looked at Sophie and felt something burning in my chest. She looked right back and then gave me a smile that was so quick I wondered if my eyes had played a trick on me.

"Upstairs, please, Aniyah!" said Mrs. Iwuchukwu, still frowning as she started to pick up the pieces of the bowl. "And, Noah, Aniyah is only going upstairs to your room so that she can have a think about what she just did, OK? She'll be back down once she's ready to say sorry for wasting a very good bowl of spaghetti. You don't need to hiccup so much, OK?"

Noah still looked frightened, but in between his hiccups, he nodded.

I wanted to scream and shout and kick something so hard it broke. But instead I looked at the floor and pushed my chair back and stood up. As I walked out of the room, I looked back over my shoulder and saw Sophie watching me. Her eyes stared straight into mine and her mouth gave another invisible grin that only I could see. I suddenly wondered if Mrs. Iwuchukwu's golden rule was also her switch, and if it was, why Sophie was making it flip, and pushing me to the wrong side of it.

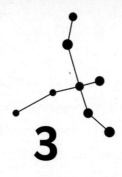

3

The Phenomenon in the Sky

After ten minutes of making me sit on my own upstairs, Mrs. Iwuchukwu sent Travis to come and get me so that I could finish eating dinner with everyone. But I wasn't going to say sorry for something I hadn't done on purpose, so I didn't. Mrs. Iwuchukwu said that meant I couldn't have dessert. I didn't want it anyway. I still wasn't hungry at all, so Sophie had mine instead. It was chocolate trifle. Which used to be my favorite.

"Sorry," said Ben quietly, after Mrs. Iwuchukwu told us we could all go and watch telly for half an hour in the living room while she cleaned up. "I didn't mean to get you into trouble."

I nodded, because it wasn't Ben's fault that Sophie didn't like me.

"Sh-shorry too," said Travis, whose eyes had grown from being the size of Ping-Pong balls to tennis balls. "Mrs. I. n-never believes us when S-Sophie does something—there's no p-point shaying anything. . . ."

"Yeah," said Ben. "And when we do, Sophie always does something worse to us—so it's best if you don't tell on her. One time she put a worm in my bed after I told Mrs. I. that it was her that had taken a five-pound note from her bag, not me."

I nodded again and sat down on one of the deep green sofas. Ben let Noah take the remote control, which made him so happy that he went and sat as close to the telly as he could, as if he was looking for a way to climb inside it. His favorite ninja cartoon that Mum always used to watch with him was just finishing.

Ben came and sat next to me on the sofa, making it bounce. Travis sat on a yellow armchair next to the coffee table and stared at me some more. I could feel my cheeks going pink again and wished they wouldn't.

"We're friends, Aniyah, yeah?" asked Ben, poking me in the arm with his elbow. "You're not angry at me, are you?"

I didn't know why, but the poking made me want to smile. So I did. Which made Travis smile too. But he quickly stopped and covered his mouth, as if he had just remembered his smile had braces in it and didn't want anyone else to know.

"So . . . how come you don't talk?" asked Ben as he looked at me with his head tilted to one side. "Do you have a stutter like Travis? Or is it because you can't?" Ben leaned forward and checked my ears to see if I had hearing aids.

I shook my head.

"There was a boy here that was like you—he came just before Christmas," said Ben. "He never spoke one word. Not even when we all got him Christmas presents! Mrs. I. told us he'd talk when he wanted to, but he didn't have anything to say yet. In the end, they had to take him away."

I looked up at Ben, feeling scared. Did "they" take him away because he wouldn't talk? Who were "they"? Where did "they" take him away to? And did he have a smaller brother and sister—and if he did, what happened to them?

"That's normal, though," said Ben. "There's always kids coming and going. That's what foster kids do—we come and then go. Usually to another foster place. That's what me and Travis had to do, until we got here. But now we want to stay here and get adopted—even if Sophie doesn't like us. It's much better to be an adopted kid than to be a foster one. But only if you haven't got any family left you want to see. Then it's better to stay fostered 'cause you can go and see them."

Travis nodded.

I opened my mouth to try to ask why they wanted to stay here and what happened when you got adopted and if that was why Sophie got to call Mrs. Iwuchukwu "mum" and they didn't. But my voice was still too far away and nothing came out.

"Mrs. I. makes the best sticky toffee pudding ever," explained Ben. "And she doesn't have any children of her own because of what happened to Mr. I., so that's why she's an extra-nice foster mum who's almost as good as a mum-mum. It'd be so cool for her to adopt us and keep us. She's much better than any of the other foster mums I've had!"

I wanted to ask what happened to Mr. Iwuchukwu and how anyone could have more than one mum, but then Travis said, "Yeah, sh-she gave us n-nice rooms. And the house is n-nicer than all the other foster onesh t-too!" His braces made his voice come out mushy, but it was better than not having one at all.

I looked around the living room and suddenly noticed all the different photos hanging on the walls. I hadn't really looked at them properly before, but in every single one of them, Mrs. Iwuchukwu was standing next to a different child. There she was standing next to a boy with bright red hair, a big nose, and even bigger glasses. And then a girl with bright yellow, curly springs for hair. Another boy in red shorts who looked like he was Asian and had straight black hair that was so shiny you could see the sunlight bouncing off it. And two twins with long brown hair who were frozen, blowing bubbles at the camera.

"Niyah . . . look!" cried Noah suddenly, turning around to me and pointing to the TV screen. But I was too busy thinking about what Ben and Travis had said about being adopted to listen to him properly. I hadn't thought that there might be lots of other kids living in lots of other foster houses too . . . and that someone could have more than one foster mum.

"Niyah! Look!" yelled Noah more loudly, bouncing up and down on his bum. *"It's mum! I found her!"*

I quickly looked at the picture Noah was pointing to on the TV. A huge ball of fire traveling through pitch-black space was being shown on one side of the screen, while on the other side, a very serious man with stiff brown hair and a frowning face was talking into a microphone.

I ran over to Noah and pressed the button on the remote control in his hand to make the volume louder.

"Astronomers have never witnessed such an enigma, and its occurrence has sparked a global race among the

world's top institutions to find any signs of similar obser-
vations in records stretching as far back as Ptolemy and
Galileo," said the man. Then his picture vanished and was
replaced by lots of images of old books and drawings with
people touching them with gloved hands. First there was a
long roll of paper covered in Chinese writing that looked
as if someone had spilled brown tea all over it, and then a
book with golden edges that had lots of drawings of men
in colorful robes and turbans looking through telescopes
with strange squiggly writing and dots surrounding the
drawings The reporter's voice came back on: "From an-
cient Chinese scrolls to the diaries of the first Arab astronomers, the search for a similar occurrence in the history of
the skies goes on. . . ."

The books began to fade away as the face of the reporter came back again—except this time, he was smiling.
"Joining me now is Professor Jasmine Grewal and astronomer Alex Withers from Royal Observatory Greenwich to
help explain this extraordinary phenomenon!"

The picture of the star on the right side of the screen
shrank as the news reporter grew and grew, until we could
all see a skinny woman in glasses with skin that was almost
as brown as mine standing next to him. Her long black
hair was being blown everywhere by the wind, and behind

her was a man with short gray hair, a spiky beard, and tiny warm brown eyes that looked all squinty, as if they couldn't open properly. Both of them were smiling too.

"Professor Grewal, let's start with you first," said the reporter, turning stiffly like a plastic doll and putting a big black microphone in front of her face. "What does this picture that we're seeing on our screens mean?"

"Well, what we're seeing, Tom, is frankly something we've never, ever seen before," said the woman, nervously smiling at the camera. "It appears to be a real live burning star moving from one end of our solar system to the other, and coming very close to our planet's atmosphere."

"That doesn't sound good!" said the reporter, staring at her with a frown, as if the star was somehow her fault. "But there must be millions of stars hurtling across our solar system! What makes this one so special?"

Looking confused, the professor turned back to the camera. "Well, no, actually, stars don't usually 'hurtle' anywhere—which is why we can count on our sun to stay where it is. It's how we can calculate light-years and navigate the skies via our constellations. Our sun is—or was until yesterday!—our nearest star and it's still nearly a hundred and fifty million kilometers away. And we know that if our sun was to come any closer, it would mean the annihilation of all life on Earth. This star has not only breached that distance by a good two million miles, but it appears to be moving through the heavens, unlike anything else we've seen!"

"So what does this mean?" questioned the reporter, looking up, as if expecting to see the star hurtling toward him. Turning to the camera with a raised eyebrow and in a voice like a game show host's, he asked, "Should the human race prepare for . . . *extinction*?"

The professor shook her head. "No, no! From our calculations of its current projected path and size, we *should* be safe from the full pull of this star's gravitational force field. Our planet could experience some very strange phenomena as a result of the immense heat the star will be radiating out at us, but because the star is new—and one of the tiniest of any newly formed stars we have ever witnessed—it should resist Earth's gravitational pull and move swiftly past. It thankfully seems to be only fractionally larger in diameter than Earth!"

I gasped and leaned closer to the telly.

The reporter nodded at the screen as if he agreed but wasn't really sure what he was agreeing with. "I see. And, Mr. Withers—why is this such a huge deal in the world of astronomy?"

The older man frowned at the reporter as if he didn't understand the question, and then looking into the camera said, "Well . . . for all the reasons Professor Grewal has just given."

The reporter nodded again and waited for Mr. Withers to say something else.

Clearing his throat, Mr. Withers leaned toward the camera and squinted even harder. "What the world has to understand is that no ball of burning gas has *ever* come closer to us than our sun. The laws of physics dictate that, one way or another, one of us would be sucked into the other's gravitational pull and destroyed. Right now, neither seems to be happening. It's just . . . passing by. And doesn't seem to be harming us at all."

"That's one super-friendly shooting star, then?" asked the reporter, looking at the TV camera while raising his eyebrow.

"Er . . ." Mr. Withers looked around as if he wished there was someone else he could talk to. "No . . . it's not a shooting star—shooting stars are pieces of rock that have actually entered our atmosphere. This phenomenon is an actual burning star."

Ignoring him, the reporter turned back to the professor. "And, Professor Grewal, what should we expect of this star next? It seems friendly now, but could it still wipe out all life on Earth?" he asked, holding the microphone to her.

Professor Grewal pushed up her glasses. "Well," she said. "All the world's observatories are now tracking its journey, and we can clearly see its progression across the northern hemisphere. But as this has never happened before, we don't know how far it will travel, or if it will change direction again, or when and where it will stop. But we can say with some certainty that it will *not* be wiping out all . . . er . . . life on Earth."

"Though that probably wouldn't be a bad thing in some cases," muttered Mr. Withers, shaking his head at the reporter.

"Niyah! Is it Mum?" whispered Noah, touching the screen where the picture of the ball of fire was. I could feel Travis and Ben standing behind us and watching us, but I didn't care.

I nodded and tried not to blink. It felt just like it did whenever Mum came to pick us up from school. Even when there were hundreds of other mums and dads in the playground, I always knew right away where Mum was—I could feel it when she was close, and sometimes I could tell it was her just by the back of her head. I'd never been wrong. Not ever. And I knew I wasn't wrong this time either.

"Thank you," said the reporter as the camera turned and zoomed in on him. "So there you have it! A universal first. A new underdog star that has defied nature's odds—and our gravitational pull—to search for its place in the heavens above. Back to you, Elaine."

The reporter disappeared and a woman in a bright purple suit sitting behind a large glass desk looked out at us instead. But the picture of the star was still behind her, so I leaned into the TV and touched it.

"Tom Bradbury there on the new phenomenon in our sky. And if you would like the chance to help the Royal Observatory name the newly discovered star, you can head over to their website at w-w-w, dot, r-m-g, dot, co, dot, u-k, forward slash, royal observatory for all the details of their brand-new competition. Next, why America's new border walls are melting in the sun."

The picture behind the newsreader changed and the star vanished. And without even knowing that it had returned, my voice cried out, *"Mum!"*

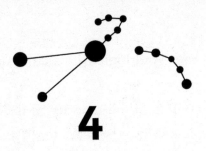

4

Mum's Star

"Jumping Jills! You *can* talk!" exclaimed Ben. I could see from his reflection in the telly that he was surprised, and that Travis was staring at my back. "But . . . why'd you call that star thing your mum?"

"Niyah! Was it really her?" whisper-asked Noah, his eyes so big and watery that I could see my whole face in them.

I nodded and turned around to look at Ben and Travis. I had to ask them something before Mrs. Iwuchukwu came into the living room, so I opened my mouth and promised my voice I'd be nice to it forever if it worked now.

"C-can I— Is there a computer in this house?" I asked. My voice felt strange—as if it didn't belong to me at all, and had gone and brought someone else's voice back instead. It sounded broken and quiet. But it didn't matter.

All that mattered was I had a voice again and I could use it to find Mum.

I needed to find the website the newsreader had talked about! I needed to know where Mum's star was exactly—and what the newsreader had meant by people helping to name it! If she was traveling across the northern hemisphere, that meant she was close by, because I knew from my star globe that we lived in the northern hemisphere too. Which meant that the constellations I could see from Mrs. Iwuchukwu's window at night would be the exact same constellations Mum's star would be traveling through right now.

Travis nodded. "I've g-got one for homework in my r-room," he said, turning bright red.

"Is it to find that website the news was talking about?" asked Ben. "About the star?"

I nodded again. Ben frowned and began to bite his bottom lip. I could tell he was asking himself a lot of questions and that he would need to get some of them out.

"But . . . but why'd you need to find out about it? And why'd you call that star 'Mum'? Your mum's not *really* a star in space! She's d—"

But before Ben could finish his sentence, Noah suddenly shouted, *"Yes she is! She* is *a star!"* then ran at Ben and gave him an angry push.

"Hey!" said Ben, looking confused and putting his hands out to stop Noah from pushing him again.

"*You say sorry!*" shouted Noah. His face turned as pink and as crinkled as the inside of a grapefruit and he began to hit Ben as hard as he could on the arm.

"Sorry! Hey, I said I'm sorry!" exclaimed Ben. "Ouch!"

I grabbed Noah's hands. "Don't hit him, Noah, he doesn't know!" I said.

"But he said it's not Mum!" cried Noah, looking at Ben with an angry frown. The curls on his head were shaking because his whole body was shaking, and his eyes were starting to get bigger and wetter.

Ben took a step back, looking confused.

Travis was frowning and making his eyeballs race around as he looked at me and then Noah and then Ben. Then quietly he said, "I'll l-let you use the c-computer . . . if you tell ush?"

Nervously rubbing his arm, Ben nodded and took a step forward. "You can tell us," he said. "We won't tell anyone, promise."

Trying to make Noah stand still, I wondered what to do. If I told them the truth, then Ben and Travis might think I was lying or being silly, because that's what people think when they don't want to believe you about something, even when it's true. I know, because Grandma Irene and Aunt Kathy used to call Mum silly, and a liar whenever she tried to tell them the truth about why all our kitchen plates were missing again, or why she had to wear sweaters with long sleeves in the summer. And one time, when a policeman came to visit our house after Dad had moved the furniture so much that he broke the kitchen table and three of the chairs, the policeman had told Mum to stop being hysterical—which I know must be another word for liar because as soon as he said it, Mum went quiet and never asked a policeman for help with the furniture ever again. But Ben and Travis weren't the police, or Grandma Irene or Aunt Kathy. There was a chance they might believe me.

I forced my throat to open again and said, "I'm a star hunter. And that star on the telly there, that's our mum. She left us to go and turn into one a few days ago—I heard her, and so did Noah. I've been trying to find her, and she's been trying to find us. And now she's shown us exactly where she is so we don't ever lose her again." Noah held my hand and, puffing up his chest like a penguin, looked up at me as if he was scared and happy all at the same time. I smiled back. I had never said those words out loud before. But now that my voice was back, it felt good to say them with my tongue and hear the sounds they made too.

It made me want to say them over and over and over again and even shout it all out! *"I'm a star hunter and I've found my mum's star!"*

"You're a *what?*" asked Ben, wrinkling his nose in confusion.

Travis pushed his hair behind his ears as if he wanted to be sure he was hearing things properly.

"A star hunter—grown-ups call them astronomers," I explained.

"Oh!" said Ben. "But you can't be an astronomer—you haven't finished school yet!" And narrowing his eyes, he looked at me as if I might be an undercover spy who was only pretending to be ten.

Travis was staring at me with his mouth open. He looked as if he had suddenly found a cave full of invisible words and didn't know what to do about it.

"You don't need to finish school to be a star hunter," I said, shaking my head and wondering if Ben and Travis had ever been to a library. "You can learn about how to become one from books and sometimes in school too."

"Oh," said Ben, frowning, but still looking as if he didn't believe me.

"And anyway, I can't wait until I finish school. I need to find Mum now so that we don't ever lose her again," I added.

"But isn't your mum . . ." Ben's frown changed from having two lines in it to three, and Travis closed his mouth and, standing up as straight as a ruler, looked at the floor. I suddenly understood what they were thinking.

"She's not *dead,*" I said, feeling angry and sorry for them all at the same time.

"She ishn't?" asked Travis, looking up, surprised.

"No. She's out there," I said, pointing through the two large glass doors of the living room.

Ben looked past my shoulder as if expecting to see a ghost, and his eyebrows began to rise like bread in an oven. "You mean . . . in the garden?"

Noah giggled and spread his hand across his face as if he couldn't believe Ben was so silly.

"No," I said, trying not to laugh too. "I mean in the sky. I already said, didn't you hear me? Mum had an extra-special heart, you see, which made it extra bright. And if you've got an extra-bright heart, when you have to leave, your heart gets taken out of your body and turned into a star so that it can watch over everyone it had to leave behind but who it didn't want to leave at all. All the best people are up there—kings and queens and millions of people who were too special to leave forever."

"You mean—like footballers and famous singers?" asked Ben, starting to look impressed.

"Yeah, maybe." I shrugged.

"Cool . . . ," said Ben, nodding as if things were starting to make sense.

"But s-stars aren't p-people. They're just balls of gash . . . ," Travis said, looking at me. I realized he might be afraid to tell me in case I got upset.

"I'm not making this up!" I promised. "I read all about it. Some of the biggest star hunters and scientists say everything's made up of dust from old stars—even us. And when we die, we get recycled too. If we're ordinary, we just go into the ground and get recycled that way. But if we're really special, we can get recycled right up there—back in space. It's actually in the *The Lion King* too," I added, suddenly wishing I could watch it again and show Ben and Travis what I meant.

"You mean the *cartoon*?" asked Ben, his mouth falling open.

I nodded, because my voice was beginning to hurt. I had made it work too hard since it got back to me, but I didn't ever want to stop using it. I gulped hard and carried on talking. "It might be a cartoon, but it's actually based on facts. In it they talk about the circle of life—and how everything is recycled—and that's all true. And how stars aren't *just* balls of gas. They need gas to keep burning, because that's their oxygen. But *all* of them have a heart," I said. "Even the ones that are so far away you can barely see them. Because after you die, if your heart is extra special, it gets thrown up into the sky and you stay there, and the rest of you goes into the ground. Why do you think all the stars have names and stories about them?"

"But that doesn't ..." Ben looked as if his mouth wasn't working anymore and there were too many questions for it to say out loud properly. "But *who's* taking out the hearts and doing all the throwing?"

"The star maker!" cried Noah, jumping up and roaring like a lion before he began running around the room.

Ben and Travis looked at him for a second and then looked back at me.

I shrugged. "I don't know. I don't have *all* the answers. And even the really old star hunters don't know that! All I know is that Mum's heart's a star now. I heard Katie say so too. She was the woman who looked after us before we came here. She said it to the policemen—that Mum belonged to the heavens now and that she was going to be looking down on us forever. And one policeman said it was a shame some people got taken so soon, but that was the way of the world. So I'm not lying."

Ben and Travis both fell quiet. I could tell they were thinking hard about everything I was saying. And I knew they wouldn't be able to argue with me, because no one could argue with scientists and star hunters. Not unless they became one. And Ben and Travis weren't star hunters like me.

Travis frowned so hard that it looked as if a caterpillar was wriggling across his forehead. After a few seconds he asked, "Wh-what does it s-sound like . . . you know? When s-someone becomesh a star?"

Noah stopped running around in circles and came and held my arm. I closed my eyes and thought about what I had heard. I could remember the noise of the explosion and how my ears had felt weird, and the strange whistling noise that had made me go deaf. And I could remember feeling dizzy because the earth under my feet seemed to be shaking, but I didn't know how to describe all that. So I just said, "Loud, and scary."

Travis nodded, and looked as if he was trying to remember something too.

"If she's . . . you know, *really* a star, what are you going to do?" asked Ben.

"I'm going to follow her," I said, and Noah nodded and pulled on my arm happily. "I have to find out which part of the sky she's going to stop in and make sure it's somewhere we can see her all the time. And where she can see us." I secretly wanted to see if Dad was following her too—because if he was, then maybe he would find Mum at the same time as we found her and he could take me and Noah home. But for some reason, I didn't want to tell Ben and Travis that.

"That's the *stupidest* thing I've *ever* heard!" said a voice from the living room door.

We all turned around and Noah stopped pulling on my arm. Sophie was standing at the doorway, running her fingers through her hair as if they were a comb. Her eyes were shining and her mouth was laughing at me. She wasn't in her school uniform anymore and was wearing jeans and a T-shirt with the faces of a pop band on it, who all looked as if they were laughing at me too.

"Your mum's *not* a star!" she said. "She's gone and she isn't *ever* coming back! She probably did it on purpose too! I would, if I knew someone as *stupid* as you!"

For three seconds after Sophie finished yelling, nothing happened. It was as if her words had made us freeze like musical statues.

Slowly, I felt my mouth open and the words *"You take that back!"* burst out, and I heard Ben and Travis saying things too and I saw Noah running over to the doorway to kick and punch Sophie in the leg.

"Ouch! *Stop that, you little brat!*" shouted Sophie, pushing him onto the floor. *"Mum! Mum! Look! Noah's gone mad! Muuuuuuuuuuuuuuum!"*

"What? What's happening here, eh?" said Mrs. Iwu-chukwu as she came running into the room with her apron half-undone.

Suddenly, Sophie screamed.

Noah had slid along the floor and angrily bitten her on the leg.

"Noah! *No!*" shouted Mrs. Iwuchukwu, pulling him away. But Noah was crying and punching and shaking too much to hear anything.

"It's—it's my fault, Mum!" said Sophie, making a sad face and looking as if she was sorry. "Maybe I said something I shouldn't have. . . ."

"Noah, stop it right *now!*" ordered Mrs. Iwuchukwu, holding him tightly in a hug-prison. "Sophie, what did you say?" she asked angrily.

"I told them I was sorry they were missing their mum, and then . . ." Sophie shrugged as she rubbed the tiny teeth marks on her leg. "He just started kicking me!"

Remembering that my voice was back and that I could tell Mrs. Iwuchukwu that Sophie was trying to flip her switch again, I opened my mouth. But instead of making any sounds, it just kept on opening and closing, like a fish looking for food.

"Niyah, she's *lying!*" cried Noah as he kicked out his

leg, trying to make it reach Sophie from where he was standing. But Mrs. Iwuchukwu was still holding his arms and Sophie was too far away.

"See?" said Sophie, tutting.

"Noah, *no*! We *never* hit or punch or kick or *bite* here!" said Mrs. Iwuchukwu, bending down so that her face was near Noah's. "*Never!* Now, Sophie didn't mean to say anything that was upsetting and she's sorry, aren't you, Sophie?"

Sophie nodded sadly, but as soon as Mrs. Iwuchukwu wasn't looking, she grinned.

Noah ran back to me and angrily wiped his eyes and face against my top.

Mrs. Iwuchukwu stood back up and looked at Noah and me, and then at Travis and Ben, who were both looking at the floor and trying not to look at anyone.

"Right! That's enough for one night! Everyone upstairs, please," said Mrs. Iwuchukwu, shaking her head at me and Noah. "Ben, Travis, finish up with your homework, then bed! Sophie—go and get started on your math homework, please. And, Noah, even though you've been a *very* naughty boy today, I know you didn't know about the no-hitting and no-biting rule. So we're going to make this the first and last time you ever do anything like that, OK?

Now. You've both got a very important day tomorrow, so off you go to bed. I'll be up in a few minutes to check on you. Chop-chop!"

Sophie ran ahead, thundering up the stairs, and slammed her door shut. But Ben and Travis silently shuffled down the corridor in front of us. I could tell they wanted to say something, but Mrs. Iwuchukwu was following us. She stopped at the bottom of the stairs and, watching us go up, said, "No loud noises—and, Travis, no computer games!" before turning back toward the kitchen door.

As we reached the corridor at the top of the stairs, Travis stopped outside the light gray door that said TRAVIS'S ROOM and, pushing his hair away from his eyes, turned around. "We'll c-come and get you later—sh-sho you can go on my c-computer," he whispered, his eyes getting wide again, as if they wanted to make sure I understood him.

"Yeah," added Ben. "After Mrs. I.'s been in to check on all of us. So don't fall asleep too early, OK?"

I nodded, and me and Noah watched them both open their bedroom doors and disappear.

"Niyah, are they our friends?" whispered Noah as we walked past Sophie's red door that had a big poster saying KEEP OUT on it, and came to a purple one with a whiteboard saying ANIYAH AND NOAH on it. The whiteboard wasn't really white anymore, because you could see pink and green smudges from all the other names that had been written before ours, and then rubbed out.

"Yeah," I said, opening the door and following Noah inside. "I think so."

After I helped get Noah ready for bed and changed into my pajamas, we both lay down so that we could pretend to be asleep when Mrs. Iwuchukwu came in. It felt just like it did at home, on one of those nights when Mum would tell us to go to bed quickly because we could hear Dad's car coming. We had to race each other and pretend we had fallen asleep right away so that Dad could see that we hadn't broken any of his bedtime rules. But Noah and me had never pretended to be asleep together, so it was more fun this time. And less scary. Especially since we knew that Mum had broken all the planet's rules to look for us, and that we weren't ever going to be left alone again.

So holding on tight to Noah and my silver locket, I squeezed my eyes shut and waited for when Ben and Travis could come and get me.

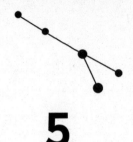

5

The Biggest Competition in the Galaxy

After Mrs. Iwuchukwu came in and told me and Noah to sleep tight and not to let any bedbugs bite us—which made Noah instantly bury his head into my arms—we waited and waited for Ben and Travis to come and get us. But after a while, Noah fell asleep, so I took out my home-made star map from inside the pillow and went and sat next to the window. Pulling the big blue curtains open, I looked straight up.

I liked that Mrs. Iwuchukwu didn't have any white gauzy curtains on any of her windows. It made being a star hunter much easier. In the hotel-that-wasn't-really-a-hotel that Mum had made us hide in, there had been hor-rible smelly, thin curtains at the window that were so dirty the white had turned yellow. They made me feel like a bee trapped in an old net. But tonight, even though the windows were super clean and there weren't any gross old curtains to have to look through, I couldn't see any stars because of the giant clouds that were in the way. Even the moon wasn't strong enough to get through them; it looked like a flashlight whose batteries needed changing.

I listened extra hard to hear if Ben or Travis were coming yet. But everything was still quiet, so I opened up my map instead and used the yellow night-light on the wall to try to guess where Mum's star might land. I hoped she would land near a constellation that was easy to spot. Like Orion's Belt or the cup with the handle on it—the Big Dipper. Maybe she could even find someone else she already knew too. Like her mum and dad. Grandma Semina and Grandpa Pedro were so special I was sure they were stars too, so maybe she could join one of them to become a binary star, which is two stars joined together, just like a proper family! I was wondering if Mum's heart might be searching for them right that very minute, when I heard a creak.

I turned around and saw the bedroom door slowly opening. I knew it wasn't Mrs. Iwuchukwu, because she never opens doors slowly. She throws them open and then floats in. I quickly folded up my map and hid it behind the curtain next to me.

"Aniyah?"

A big round blob of fluffy hair came around the edge of the door, followed by the large white circles of Ben's eyes.

"I'm near the window," I whispered back, standing up. Now that my voice was back again and I didn't feel like a fish anymore, everything felt much easier.

"Come on!" he whispered, quickly checking over his shoulder.

I looked at Noah to see if he was still asleep. I felt bad for going without him, but he had one leg lifted in the air and was breathing loudly. I knew that he was in a deep sleep, so I decided not to wake him.

Ben waited as I tiptoed over to the door. He put a finger to his lips. "We have to make sure Sophie doesn't hear us," he whispered. "Or she'll get us into trouble."

I nodded and, copying his footsteps as he tried to avoid the creaky floorboards, carefully followed him to Travis's room. I had never been inside anyone else's room but ours and hadn't really thought about what they might be like. The room Mrs. Iwuchukwu had given me and Noah to sleep in was nice, but it wasn't even a little bit as cool as Travis's room was.

Travis's room was like a museum—a museum for comic books and superhero toys! The walls were a silvery gray color that made me feel like we were inside a spaceship, and there were lots of posters of a cartoon boy with big eyes, a small nose, and brown-and-yellow hair standing underneath the word *Hikaru* printed in giant zigzag writing. There was a huge bookcase on the wall opposite his desk filled with hundreds of comic books and lots of tiny figures of different superheroes. I thought it was one of the best bedrooms I had ever seen, and it made me wonder what Ben's room was like too.

"I'm not s-supposed to use the c-computer after l-lights-out," said Travis as he quietly waved me over. "Sho you can't tell anyone! P-promish!"

I nodded and said, "I promise!"

Sitting down at his shiny black computer table, Travis quickly typed in his password. I tried not to look, but I could see right away that the password was "TravisHik123." It made me think of Dad, because I knew he would have shaken his head and told Travis to change it to a harder one. Dad's computer had a password that was at least as long as half of the whole alphabet and was so hard that even he forgot it sometimes.

After a picture of the Hikaru cartoon boy came up on the screen, Travis opened a web browser and typed the words:

Immediately, a long list of websites came up. Travis clicked on the first one. It was a short news article about Mum's star.

"No," I said. "That doesn't say anything about where the star is going. Maybe we should try to find out about the competition the news lady was talking about?"

Travis nodded and tried a different search:

new star name competition

This time the results were all about how to buy a star or enter baby-naming competitions.

"Why would anyone have a competition to name their baby?" asked Ben, shaking his head as he took out a biscuit from his hoodie and munched on it loudly.

"Can we try the website the news lady said?" I asked.

"C-can you remember it?" asked Travis.

I nodded and, closing my eyes, made my brain remember the news lady's voice and the words she said, and then repeated them with my mouth. Travis typed the address in:

www.rmg.co.uk/royalobservatory

In less than a second, a screen with the most exciting words I had ever seen stared out at us in big bold letters:

**ENTER THE BIGGEST COMPETITION
IN THE GALAXY AND HELP US NAME
A NEW STAR!**

<<CLICK HERE TO LEARN MORE>>

"Wow!" whispered Ben as Travis quickly clicked the link. Another page burst open, and right there, at the very top of it, was a huge photograph of Mum's star burning through space. It felt like a balloon was expanding right in the middle of my chest, and my nose started to tickle, and I knew it was because I was feeling proud of Mum. She had been looking for me and Noah so hard that she had made herself famous!

Travis scrolled down. Below the picture of Mum's star were two boxes—one with a number in it that was going down one digit at a time, and one with a number in it that kept jumping up in ways that no one could guess. When we first looked at the second number, it said 23,221. Then a moment later, it said 23,428. Then 23,512.

We all leaned in as Ben read the page out loud.

THREE DAYS TO BE A PART
OF SPACE HISTORY!

Royal Observatory Greenwich proudly
invites you to help us name the world's first-
ever close-encounter star phenomenon!
At 14:28:15 GMT on Thursday 29th October,
our astronomers were the first to spot what
appeared to be a newly born star blazing
across the solar system. Already noted for
its dangerous proximity to planet Earth,
this seemingly ordinary star has, instead
of directly heading for Earth's surface,
defied the laws of physics to pull itself
back out into the farther corners of
outer space!
To honor this extraordinary marvel and
mark a first in the history of astronomy, we
are giving the world's citizens the unique
chance of naming this new star as it takes
its place in the Milky Way.

TO ENTER

Simply complete the form «HERE» before the final deadline, telling us the name you would like to give to the star and why. All names *must* be limited to one word only. While names may come from any part of the world, all entries must be spelled using the English alphabet.

Only one entry per person.

For all persons aged sixteen years old and under wishing to enter, a guardian/parent name and email address are required.

Deadline: All entries must be submitted by 00:00, Sunday 1st November.

THE SELECTION OF THE WINNING NAME

After the competition closes, the winning entry will be randomly selected by our computers. The announcement of the winning name, which will be televised live around the world at 19:00, Sunday 1st November, will take place at the Kronos

Gala. This prestigious event marks the 250th year since the establishment of Kronos Watches and will take place at the Peter Harrison Planetarium in Greenwich, London. The entrant with the winning name will be duly informed by email and awarded a unique naming certificate, together with a special limited-edition Kronos timekeeper.

At the bottom of the page was a large photograph of a scroll tied with a black ribbon, and the most beautiful watch I had ever seen. It had a navy-blue face with silver numbers going all the way around it and lots of tiny stars shining out around the edge. But instead of its hands being ordinary and straight and pointy, the large hand was a silver shooting star, and the small hand was a crescent moon. And in tiny golden writing in the middle of the watch were the words *Kronos 250*.

"Whoa!" said Travis. "That's the b-best watch I've ever sh-sheen!"

"Yeah!" Ben said, nodding. "It's like the ones James Bond wears in the films!" Suddenly falling silent, he looked out the window and stared into space. I think he was imagining himself wearing the watch.

Travis scrolled back up to the top of the page. "B-but

look how many people have s-sent their namesh in already!" he said, pointing at the second number, which had now jumped up to 24,112.

Ben leaned over Travis's shoulder and shook his head. "And there's still fifty-one hours to go!"

Looking at the second number, I suddenly realized what it meant and felt a hard thump in my chest. "But—but they can't let someone else name Mum's star!" I said. "We've got to let them know that she's already got a name!"

Travis scrolled down the page to where the form was. "We could f-fill in the form and tell them," he suggested.

Ben shook his head. "They won't see it—they'll probably get a hundred million forms in! It's a competition for the whole *galaxy*, remember?"

Travis nodded. "W-wait a minute!" he said as he scrolled down the page. At the very bottom, in the part of the page that turned black, was a list. Travis leaned in and clicked on the words that said *Contact Us*. "Maybe we can r-ring them tomorrow when Mrs. I. ishn't l-looking," he suggested.

But when the new page opened, there was only a map showing where the observatory was, and an email address. There wasn't a single phone number anywhere.

"Let's email them!" said Ben. "Me and Travis have both got emails now! We could send one each!"

I shook my head. "Look," I said, pointing to a small line of writing underneath the email address.

Travis and Ben both leaned in as Travis read the line out loud.

"All general in-q-quiry emails will be responded to within s-seven daysh. If you would like to c-contact a known member of s-staff, you may do so u-using first, dot, last name, at, r-o-g, dot, c-o, dot, u-k."

"Bleeding lightbulbs! That's rubbish," said Ben, biting his lip. "We don't know any members of staff . . . and we can't wait for seven days!"

"Aniyah, do you remember the p-professor's name?" asked Travis, looking up at me hopefully. "The one from the n-news? Like you r-remembered the website addresh?"

"Oh yeah! Because she's a member of staff!" said Ben, giving Travis a clap on the back. "Well done!"

I squeezed my eyes shut and tried to remember. I could see her long black hair and the color of her glasses and the way her face had looked when the news reporter asked her questions. But I couldn't remember her whole name. . . .

I shook my head. "Just that she was a Professor Gray-something."

"What we gonna do now, then?" asked Ben, looking at us hopelessly.

We all stared silently at the screen as Travis clicked the Back button and opened up the competition page again. Suddenly, I felt my brain jump up and bang itself against the roof of my head. It had the answer!

"I know! We can just *go* to where the star hunters are! They're in London, so they can't be that far!"

I looked at Ben and Travis and waited for them to get excited too. But instead, they just frowned.

"We've n-never been to London," said Travis.

"Yes you have," I said, wondering what was wrong with both of them. "We're in London right now."

Ben shook his head. "No, that's where you *used* to live, maybe. With your mum and dad. Before . . ."

I looked at Ben and Travis and wondered if they might be trying to play a trick on me. But they looked so serious that it made my head start to feel dizzy. I tried to think. The night Mum had picked me and Noah up from school and told us we were going to play hide-and-seek with Dad, she had made us get into a taxi, and the taxi had driven us for a long time. I knew it was a long time, because I fell asleep, and when I woke up, the sun had disappeared. I knew that Mum's last game of hide-and-seek had hidden us from Dad, but I didn't know that it had hidden us from London too! And the woman in the black suit hadn't said anything about where the foster house was or how far it was from our real home. All she had kept saying was that everything was going to be fine!

"Where—where are we?" I asked. I could feel my voice shaking as if it was getting ready to run away again.

Ben and Travis stayed silent and looked at each other with a question on their faces. I could feel something wet running down my nose, so I angrily wiped it away.

Then Ben said, "Waverley Village," quietly, as if he was feeling sorry for me.

"N-near Oxford," added Travis.

I had heard of Oxford because of the dictionary, but I didn't know where it was, so I didn't know what to think.

"It's pretty far from L-London," explained Travis, before falling quiet again.

I squeezed my eyes shut and tried to stop them from stinging me. But I couldn't, and suddenly my face was wet and my nose was running too.

"Don't cry, Aniyah," said Ben, putting a hand out and patting me on the shoulder. "It'll be all right. I felt like that when I first came here too."

"Yeah," said Travis, rubbing the side of his nose as if it suddenly needed to be polished. "I u-used to live by the b-beach with my m-mum. It was hard moving here. . . ."

I nodded and, feeling embarrassed, wiped my face with the back of my pajama sleeves.

I looked at Ben and Travis and opened my mouth, but my voice had disappeared again. Instead, I tried to tell them with my eyes that it didn't matter one bit how far away from London we were, or how hard it was going to be to get a message to the star hunters! The computer said I had over fifty-one hours to stop them from giving Mum's star the wrong name. So that's exactly what I was going to do.

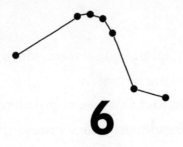

6

Time's Tricks

At breakfast the next morning, while Mrs. Iwuchukwu was making toast and dancing, Ben and Travis kept whispering to each other and then looking at me. I wondered what they were talking about until Ben leaned across the table and, using his hands to make a mouth-cave, whispered, "Aniyah, we're going to have another meeting tonight . . . about you-know-what! OK?"

I nodded, because I had lots I wanted to tell them too.

"Look!" whispered Travis. Leaning forward and looking around to make sure Sophie wasn't near, he gave me a piece of paper. I quickly unrolled the note and read it. There weren't any words on it, only some scribbled numbers. It said:

40:35:11   1,089,247

Time was running out.

"What's that?" asked Sophie. Noah had been banging his spoon against the table loudly and talking to himself about all the things he was going to eat for breakfast, so none of us had heard her come in.

I quickly squashed the note up in my hands and pushed it into my trouser pocket, waiting for her to say something. Even Noah had stopped talking and was watching her as if he knew she was dangerous too. But she just narrowed her eyes and, flicking her ponytail, said, "Whatever!" before sitting down in her chair.

"Here we are!" sung Mrs. Iwuchukwu as she put a large plate of hot toast smothered with gooey chocolate spread and topped with small round banana slices on the table. "Friday choco-banana toasties! You can't say I don't spoil you, eh?"

Ben and Travis instantly grabbed one each and shoved them into their mouths as if they hadn't eaten anything for a year. Noah started bouncing up and down in excitement. I put one on his plate for him and watched as he began poking his tongue out like a lizard to lick the bananas.

"Aniyah?" asked Mrs. Iwuchukwu. "You too. You really do need to start eating properly, darling, or I'll have to take you to the doctor's. We don't do underfed in this house!"

I nodded and put a slice on my plate. I wanted to make Mrs. Iwuchukwu happy so that she would tell me how far away Waverley was from London. And for the first time since Mum left, I was feeling hungry.

"Thank you, Mrs. Iwu-Iwuchukwu," I said, taking a bite.

"Oh my! What's this?" cried Mrs. Iwuchukwu, staring at me and then looking around at everyone. "You're *talking*! Aniyah! Your voice is back!" Clapping her hands and jumping up to give me a hug, she said, "Oh, that's wonderful! We'll have to celebrate properly tonight, eh? Your caseworker will be so happy when we tell her today!"

Travis and Ben smiled secretly at me as Noah cried out, "Yeah, yeah, yeah!" and banged his spoon on the table even harder. I had forgotten that Mrs. Iwuchukwu hadn't heard me speak yesterday, so I smiled too. It would be easier for me to ask all my questions and get the answers I needed when Mrs. Iwuchukwu was happy with me.

"Mum, don't be silly!" said Sophie, gulping down her toast. "She's been speaking since yesterday! I heard her. But she's been hiding it from you!"

"Oh . . . ," said Mrs. Iwuchukwu, her smile suddenly getting smaller.

I looked across the table at Sophie. She wasn't grinning, but I could tell she was laughing at me from the inside.

"Well! It's still the best news!" said Mrs. Iwuchukwu, trying to act as happy as she had been before. "Us foster mums don't need to know everything right away, now, do we? Eh?"

I didn't know what to say, so I looked at Sophie and gave her my first-ever I-hate-you stare. I had never given one to anyone—not even to Stupid Steven at school, who liked calling me and Noah "half-baked buns" because Mum was from Brazil and Dad was English. But I must have done the stare wrong, because instead of making Sophie frown or look sad, it made her smile a smile that lasted right until she picked up her bag and left for school.

After Ben and Travis had left for school too and I had finished a whole piece of toast, Mrs. Iwuchukwu told me to take Noah upstairs and get our coats from the wardrobe, because she was going to take us out.

"You mean out-out?" I asked, suddenly feeling excited. We had only been in the garden since coming to the foster house, but that had a wall all the way around it, so it didn't count.

"Yes," said Mrs. Iwuchukwu, nodding and smiling. "Out-out. We're going to meet your caseworker today and a very special police officer. Go and get ready, please! Quickly. We're already running a little bit late."

I took Noah by the hand and went upstairs, not

feeling so excited anymore. I didn't know what a "case-worker" was, but it didn't sound like it would be someone fun. And I didn't like police officers, no matter how special they were, because after we started hiding in the hotel-that-wasn't-really-a-hotel, Mum would always cry after she had been to see one. But if we were going outside, then I could see where we were, and if there was a train station that had trains to London nearby.

After I helped Noah put his coat and shoes on, Mrs. Iwuchukwu helped us into her car and began to drive. At first she drove us down a long, curvy road with lots of different-colored houses on it. But then the houses disappeared, and the road got thinner, and narrower, and tinier, until it was so small that whenever a car came the other way, Mrs. Iwuchukwu had to stop to let it go by. I had never seen such a squished road before, and I couldn't remember seeing it when the woman in the black suit had brought us.

After a while, the road got bigger again, until we were in a town with lots of cars and people and buildings all made out of the same golden-brown stone. I pressed my nose up against the window and tried to read the signs. But there weren't any that pointed to London, and I couldn't see a sign for a train station anywhere either.

"Here we are!" said Mrs. Iwuchukwu as we turned into a small road and stopped next to a big building that had the words OXFORD CHILDREN'S SERVICES written on the front of it in giant white letters.

"Niyah, look!" said Noah, pointing out of the car window to a large slide that was painted to look like a caterpillar in front of the building. "Can we play there? Pleeeeeeeeease!" he begged, clapping his hands as Mrs. Iwuchukwu helped him out of the car. But she shook her head and, holding out her hand, said, "Not now, Noah—but I'll let you play afterward if you promise to be good, OK?"

Noah nodded and, for the first time ever, let her hold his hand.

I didn't want to hold Mrs. Iwuchukwu's hand, but she didn't seem to mind, and she let me follow her and Noah into the building.

"Mrs. Iwuchukwu?" asked a woman as we went up to the reception desk. She had a sweater with a sparkling panda bear on it and coils of yellow hair that looked like pasta twists and eyes that were bright blue. And next to her was a tall woman in a white shirt and black trousers, with hair that was plaited into a big rope. She was wearing silver glasses that were as round as her eyes, and that made her look like a robot.

Mrs. Iwuchukwu nodded.

"Ah! I'm Ms. Trevors and this is Detective Carolyn Lewis from the CID. And this must be Noah and Aniyah," said the woman, bending down. She held out her hand and waited for me to shake it, and then for Noah to shake it too.

"If you'll follow us," said Ms. Trevors, smiling and leading us all into a small room where everything was gray. The only thing that wasn't gray was a table where there was a packet of coloring pens, some paper, and a box full of Lego bricks.

"Now, Aniyah and Noah, normally I wouldn't see you both for a good couple of weeks so that you have some time to settle down into your new home with Mrs. Iwuchukwu," said Ms. Trevors, letting Noah run over to the Lego box and start playing. "And I know that your family liaison officer and Mrs. Granger would have told you that I would be meeting you soon too. . . ." She looked at me and Mrs. Iwuchukwu as we both sat down on a long gray sofa, and she and the stiff detective woman sat down on two chairs opposite us. I tried to remember who the people she was talking about were, but I couldn't.

"But right now, Detective Lewis and I need a little help to understand some of the things that happened before your mum . . . left. And we need to ask you some questions. Is that OK, Aniyah?"

Ms. Trevors and the detective robot lady and Mrs. Iwuchukwu all stared at me and waited for me to say something.

My voice had vanished again, so I just nodded and sat on my hands because they suddenly felt like blocks of ice.

"Good girl," said Ms. Trevors. "Now, you don't have to answer any question that you don't want to, and if you find it too hard to tell me something, you can write it down for me—or draw it for me with these. OK?"

I nodded again as Ms. Trevors put some sheets of plain paper and coloring pens next to me and then looked up at the large plastic clock on the wall. Travis's piece of paper had said we only had forty hours left to find a way to stop the star hunters at the Royal Observatory from naming Mum's star wrong. But that was over an hour ago, so now we only had thirty-nine. . . .

Ms. Trevors looked at a clipboard and began asking me lots of questions from it. I had heard some of them before from Katie, Mum's friend from the hotel-that-wasn't-really-a-hotel. They were about Mum and Dad and what kinds of games Dad liked playing with us. Like the Home-Time Game—which was when me and Mum and Noah had to race home after school every day and be there by exactly four o'clock so that we could pick up the phone when Dad rang. It didn't matter how far away Dad was, or even if he was in another country for work, he always rang at exactly four o'clock to make sure we were all home and had stayed safe. And the Disappearing Sorry Game. That was a game Dad played when he had broken something—like a plate or a chair—or if Mum had fallen over when he was moving the furniture. We knew he was playing it because he would disappear for hours and come back with flowers and toys and chocolates and presents and try to say sorry at least fifty times in an hour. There were lots of other games too, but I didn't feel like talking about them out loud, so I wrote some of them down instead. It's tiring having to answer the same questions over and over again, so I didn't give long answers, only short ones.

But then the detective robot lady started asking me brand-new questions I had never been asked before—all about the day Mum left. I could feel my hand stop writing and my eyes starting to sting. Because the truth is, I can't remember everything that happened that day. Not properly anyway. And it makes me feel scared. I don't ever want to forget the last day I saw Mum, but whenever I try to remember what she looked like or what she was wearing or what she said to me, my brain goes fuzzy and I start to get worried that I'll forget everything about her. It makes me think of a story Mum once read to me about Father Time, and how he could play tricks on people he didn't like.

In the story, Father Time became angry at the human world for wasting all his gifts on trying to make time into money and starting wars. So to punish them, he made all the clocks of the world go faster and faster and faster, until no one could remember the people they loved, or their happiest memories, or understand how they had suddenly become old and gray in the blink of an eye. Only children who knew how to spend their time happily were saved. To stop Father Time from being cruel, all you had to do was be as happy as you could be, for as long as you could be, and be grateful for every minute you were given. Because as soon as you stopped, Father Time would make the clocks speed up and make you old and forgetful and sad in a blink of an eye. I guess I must have done something wrong on the day Mum disappeared, because time keeps stretching itself out or disappearing, and makes all the pictures in my head go blurry—like a new painting that someone's accidentally spilled water over.

The things I *can* remember from the day Mum disappeared are these:

I remember waking up and seeing Mum brushing her teeth in the tiny sink in the corner of the room we were sleeping in, and putting her hair up into a ponytail. She had stopped keeping her hair straight and perfect for Dad, so it had become all curly and springy, just like mine and Noah's. She had stopped wearing makeup too, because she said she didn't have to look pretty all the time anymore, but I thought that she looked even prettier without it.

Then I can remember getting out my "undercover clothes" for the day. That's what we called all the clothes at the hotel-that-wasn't-really-a-hotel, because they'd come from a giant trash bag and weren't really ours. They were clothes someone had given us to wear so that no one would recognize us and we could win the game of hide-and-seek with Dad.

I remember getting dressed and asking Mum if I looked OK, and seeing her put down the big pile of papers she was holding in her hands. They were papers to help us hide better, and they made Mum look sad and worried. I remember asking if I could help her with the papers and Mum smiling back at me. Mum had the most beautiful smile in the whole world, because whenever she smiled, it made everyone else around her smile too. I remember feeling happy and hoping my teeth would be just as white and as shiny as hers one day. I think Mum said something back to me, but when I try to remember what she said, it suddenly goes blurry and— *whooooooooooooosh!*—time skips everything that happened at breakfast and what Mum had looked like when she made me and Noah our last crumpets, and fast-forward to Mum taking us into the playroom.

I remember Felicity, our babysitter, opening the door and saying hello to us, and Mum telling Noah not to be naughty. I can remember Mum's hair tickling my face as she bent down to give me a kiss, and the sound of her voice as she said, "I'll see you both later. Be good. And don't forget to eat your vegetables at lunch!" And if I try very hard and squeeze my eyes shut and make my ears stop listening, I can even remember seeing Mum wave at me, and how bright her eyes had sparkled and the way her nose had wrinkled up a little when she said goodbye. But then the image goes blurry again, and with another *whoooooooooooooooooosh!* time skips most of the day and only throws me small pieces of pictures like broken bits of a mirror. Like:

1. The playroom suddenly becoming empty because all the other children had left
2. Katie looking at her watch and being on her phone and shaking her head and saying the words "I can't get through"
3. The small garden outside the house getting darker and darker and darker . . .

Then *whooooooooooooooooooosh!*

Time speeds up again and comes to a stop at exactly eight o'clock. I know it was that time precisely, because when Katie opened the TV room door it made me look up at the clock. I thought Mum was going to be with her. But it wasn't Mum at all—it was two police officers instead, and both of them had large watery eyes that stared straight into mine.

The very last thing I remember is watching the hands of the clock on the wall, and the small hand standing still above the number eight as if it didn't want to move. In this part, my memory plays even more tricks on me, because it made sound fade away and words become jumbled—as if everything was being squashed and sucked up by a giant silent vacuum. The only words that my ears can remember hearing are: "Family . . . officer . . . Your mum wanted . . . Gone . . . Do you . . . So sorry . . . Understand . . . Got to leave . . ."

I can't remember who said those words, or what the missing words were, or whose hands put themselves on my shoulders and made me turn cold. All I know is—that was when I heard a loud crack from somewhere deep inside my chest, and a large explosion taking place high up in the skies, and a creaking as if the world had stopped turning and didn't know how to move again. I looked around to see if Felicity or Katie or the police officers had heard the noises too, but their mouths were still going up and down, so I knew they hadn't, because no one who had heard those noises could go on talking. Then I looked down at

Noah, who was staring up at me, his face red and wet and his mouth open, and I knew right away that he had heard the same sounds. They were the sounds of Mum's heart leaving her body and becoming a star.

But I couldn't write any of this down, and I didn't want to tell Ms. Trevors or the robot detective woman that I couldn't remember things clearly. I waited until they got bored of asking me questions and asked me the one question I had been wanting to hear.

"So, Aniyah . . . is there anything you'd like to ask me— or Detective Lewis?"

I looked up at Ms. Trevors and opened my mouth. I could feel my throat trying to unlock itself again and waited for the sounds to come out. After a few seconds, I heard myself ask, "How far away are we from London?"

Ms. Trevors frowned at me and then at the detective and then at Mrs. Iwuchukwu. "Well, I know that you used to live in London, so it's perfectly normal that you'd like to know," she said, quickly writing something on her clipboard. "You're only an hour away by train, a little longer by coach or car—not too far away, Aniyah. When things are a little more settled, Mrs. Iwuchukwu can take you down for a trip?"

Mrs. Iwuchukwu nodded.

"Anything else?"

I wanted to ask her at least fifty more questions. Like where Dad was and if he knew where we were now, or if he had given up trying to find us. And if living in a foster house meant that I couldn't ever go home again. And if we weren't ever going back, what was going to happen to my star globe, and all my books, and my favorite Halloween costume, and Noah's favorite light-up sneakers, and the toy Woody that helped him sleep at night?

But instead I shook my head and looked back up at the clock on the wall. Another hour had gone, which meant I only had thirty-eight left now. The thought made my heart want to run. But I wouldn't let it. Because no matter how many tricks time played on me from now on, I wasn't going to let it take anything away from me ever again.

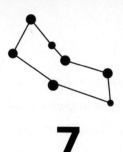

7

The Secret Detective

When we got home from the children's services building, Mrs. Iwuchukwu let me and Noah play in the living room while she got a pizza ready for lunch. She put on the radio extra loud because it was Friday, and sang a weird song that made her sound like she was being strangled. The radio said it was "opera hour," which I guess is a special hour for people who can't sing to try to sing as loud as they can.

While Noah was busy pretending to have a car chase with the big box of toy cars Mrs. Iwuchukwu had given him, I started thinking about what Ms. Trevors had said—that London was only a train or coach ride away. But when we had been driving back to the house and went through the town with all the old church buildings again, I had looked as hard as I could for a train station and tried to see if there were any coaches anywhere too. But all I had seen was a sign that said THANK YOU FOR VISITING THE HISTORICAL TOWN OF OXFORD and lots of cars and people on bicycles.

And then suddenly, I had a brain wave!

All I needed was a bike! If Travis or Ben had one and let me borrow it, I could cycle my way to the star hunters who were naming Mum's star! It might take me a little bit longer than getting the train or a coach, but I didn't have any money for them anyway, and I was good at cycling. When Dad had taught me, he had called me "a natural."

As soon as my brain had finished waving at me, I decided to ask Mrs. Iwuchukwu as many questions as I could without her knowing that I was asking anything important at all. At home, whenever Dad was away working in another country for his bank and Mum could do whatever she wanted, she would wrap herself up in a blanket and watch a detective show about a man with a funny accent and an even funnier mustache. He would always ask questions that were clever because they seemed simple but weren't really, and after he finished asking them, he would nod and stroke his mustache. That was how he always found the answers and won his cases. So that's what I was going to do too—I was going to be just like the detective and get all the answers I needed without anyone guessing that's what

I was doing. And since I didn't have a mustache, I would stroke my eyebrows instead.

Leaving Noah playing, I went into the kitchen. Mrs. Iwuchukwu was cutting up some tomatoes next to the sink and shaking her bright green dress to the music from the radio. From behind, she looked like the top of a tree being moved around by the wind. After a few seconds, she turned around and, jumping back, put a hand on her heart and said, "Oh, Aniyah! I didn't see you there! You almost gave me a heart attack!" It was exactly what the people on Mum's TV show did whenever they saw the detective, so I knew I was doing the detecting right.

"Mrs. Iwu-Iwuchukwu? Is there a bike I can play with?"

"You mean ride? Right now?" Mrs. Iwuchukwu frowned and turned to look outside the window. There were gray clouds rolling by slowly and dots of water on the glass.

"Well, it's a little cold today, Aniyah, and it looks like the rains are starting, so maybe tomorrow, eh?"

"But—but there *is* a bike that I can use?" I asked, trying to make my face stay the same and not look too excited.

"Well, there's no reason why you can't borrow Travis's or Ben's, or even Sophie's bike." She smiled. "They're in the shed, so we can get them out when it gets a little sunnier. I'll have to see if I can get you a helmet too."

I nodded, and then, remembering what the detective

did, I stroked both my eyebrows. Outside, my face didn't change even a little bit, but inside, my brain was jumping up and down on a trampoline and punching the air and crying out, *Yesssss!*

I didn't want Mrs. Iwuchukwu to guess what I was doing, so I decided I would wait for a half hour before I asked her my next secret question. The detective on the show never asked all his questions in one go, in case the suspects started to get suspicious, so I would ask her something else when she wasn't expecting any questions at all. And if I waited and only asked her something every half hour, I would have found out at least three things before Ben and Travis came home from school!

As soon as I made the decision to wait for a half hour, time began to go so slowly that I was sure it was broken. But I wasn't going to give up, so I went and drew with Noah, and then I helped Mrs. Iwuchukwu set the table, and then I ate my pizza extra slowly, and then I slurped my orange juice even slower, until, finally, a half hour passed by.

Putting my glass down, I wiped my mouth with the back of my hand. Noah was copying me and giggling, so he did the same thing and waited to see what I would do next.

"Mrs. Iwuchukwu?"

Mrs. Iwuchukwu finished taking a bite of her pizza and said, "Yes?"

"Do you like road maps?"

Again, just like the people on the detective show, Mrs. Iwuchukwu looked surprised, so I knew I had asked it right. "Well, no . . . I can't say I do. . . . I usually just use my satnav to get around. Do you want to see it?"

I nodded and watched as Mrs. Iwuchukwu went over to the kitchen window, where her red radio was, and unplugged something from its charger.

"It's old now, but Mr. Iwuchukwu loved using it. Here," she said, switching it on and holding it out to me.

I had never held a real satnav before, because Mum and Dad's ones had been fixed to the inside of their cars and had never needed to be plugged into a wall to be charged. It was like a tiny black TV screen and a computer-game console all mixed into one. Noah leaned over my shoulder as the screen flashed on for a second and then quickly went black again.

"Oh dear! I forgot to put the switch on," said Mrs. Iwuchukwu, taking the satnav back and plugging it in again. "I'm awful at charging these things!"

"Oh," I said, wondering if Travis could find the map I needed online instead and print me a copy.

"But I do also have a *London A to Z . . . ,*" she said, sitting back down at the table and wiping her mouth with a napkin. Noah had stopped copying me and was copying

Mrs. Iwuchukwu instead, so he picked up his napkin as well. Only instead of wiping just his mouth, he started wiping his whole face with it.

I wondered what she meant by a *London A to Z,* and if Mrs. Iwuchukwu had accidentally thought I meant a dictionary instead of a map. But then she said, "I still take it with me when I'm driving somewhere new in London. Sometimes even satnavs get it wrong, so it's always best to have a backup! Why? Do you like road maps, Aniyah?"

Mrs. Iwuchukwu was looking at me with her head tilted to one side, which made her look like Ben.

I nodded.

"Well, that's very interesting. I don't think I know anyone who likes road maps!"

"So can I . . . can I look inside the *London A to Z?*" I asked, feeling my feet getting excited under the table.

"Of course." Mrs. Iwuchukwu smiled. "It's on one of the shelves in the living room somewhere. You can borrow it anytime you want."

My brain did another jump on its trampoline as I nodded and stroked my eyebrows and forced myself not to ask any more questions.

After lunch, Mrs. Iwuchukwu found the *London A to Z* map book for me. It was a strange book, with hundreds of pages of yellow roads and green blobs and numbers and lines and squares with letters running along the top. I had seen maps like it before in old school textbooks, but I didn't know how I was supposed to use it to get to the star hunters to stop them from giving Mum's star the wrong name. I decided Travis would need to find me an easier map on his computer and that I would give Mrs. Iwuchukwu back her confusing *London A to Z.*

As I pretended to look through it so that Mrs. Iwuchukwu would think that I really was enjoying it, I thought extra hard about how to ask my final question. I had to try to think of a different way of saying the word *flashlight.* But no matter how hard I thought about it, no other words seemed good enough. I couldn't ask Mrs. Iwuchukwu for a shining stick of light or a light machine. It wouldn't make any sense, and it made me realize that there are just some words that can't ever be replaced by other ones and still mean the same thing. In the end, just as Mrs. Iwuchukwu was showing Noah how to make his fingers click as loud as the people were doing on the telly, I asked, "Mrs. Iwuchukwu—can I have a flashlight . . . please?"

Mrs. Iwuchukwu looked at me and raised her eyebrows. "A flashlight?" she asked.

I nodded. I could see she was thinking something

serious, so my mouth suddenly said a lie. I didn't even know what it was saying until I heard myself say the words "I don't like sleeping in the dark without one."

I could feel my face beginning to go red, because it didn't like lying. I had never slept with a flashlight before, so my face couldn't pretend that I had. But I needed the flashlight to get to Mum's star, and I knew Mum would say it was OK to tell this lie because it would help keep me safe and stop Mrs. Iwuchukwu from worrying about me. Mum always told lies to lots of people to stop them from worrying about us and it always made her go red in the face too.

Mrs. Iwuchukwu tapped her chin with her finger, and after a few seconds said, "Well, I'm sure I have a travel flashlight somewhere. I'll see if I can find it for you, OK?"

I nodded and went back to pretending to read the *London A to Z* again. I had asked all my questions and I didn't need to do any more detecting now. As soon as Ben and Travis got home, I would tell them all about my plan and ask if I could borrow one of their bikes—and a helmet too. I would need them to help me get out of the house and maybe learn how to use the map, but so long as I did that by tomorrow night, I could make it before time ran out and the competition for naming Mum's star was over.

But Ben and Travis didn't come home at three-forty like they usually did. Or at four o'clock. Or even at five o'clock! I wanted to ask Mrs. Iwuchukwu where they were and what was making them late, because I didn't like people going missing when they were meant to be home already and it was starting to make me feel sick.

But then, at exactly five-forty-one, the front door opened and I heard Ben's and Travis's footsteps running down the corridor.

"Boys! Dinner first!" cried Mrs. Iwuchukwu as they both burst into the kitchen wearing muddy T-shirts and shorts.

"Wicked! Burger and chips!" said Ben as he leaped into his chair and grabbed a burger from the big plate in the middle of the table. "Al-wigh, Aniyah. Al-wigh, Noah!" he added as he stuffed great big bites into his cheeks until they looked ready to burst.

I nodded as Noah poked me on the arm to ask for a burger too.

"Be sure to leave some chips for Sophie!" said Mrs. Iwuchukwu as she came and put an oven tray of chips in front of us. "She'll be starving after swimming practice."

Ben and Travis nodded as they each grabbed another burger and gulped it down in under thirty seconds.

Chewing like a camel and gulping hard, Ben pushed a handful of chips into his mouth and suddenly jumped up. "Mrs. I., I'm gon go 'ave m'shower!" he shouted.

"All right," said Mrs. Iwuchukwu from the cooker, where the loud hissing noise of something frying could be heard.

"Me t-too!" said Travis, standing up and noisily scraping his chair back from the table.

"Psst! Aniyah! Come to Travis's room after you've finished dinner, OK?" whispered Ben, leaning across the table.

"OK," I whispered back.

"We've got s-something to show you!" said Travis, looking excited. And licking bits of chips from the front of his braces, he gave me a thumbs-up and quickly raced Ben out the kitchen door.

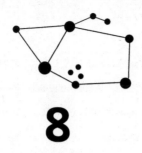

8

The Star Hunters' Top-Secret Midnight Mission!

"Have you finished, Aniyah?" asked Mrs. Iwuchukwu as I quickly slid down from my chair and stood up next to the dinner table.

I nodded, hoping that the leaving-the-table-whenever-you-wanted rule would be the same for me as it seemed to be for Ben and Travis and Sophie.

Mrs. Iwuchukwu looked down at my plate and the half-eaten burger that sat in the middle of it. I had tried to finish it, but my throat had closed its doors again. It was too excited to find out what Travis and Ben wanted to show me to let any more food go in.

"Hmmm," said Mrs. Iwuchukwu, frowning. "I think you'll have to have some milk later. Eh?"

I nodded again and opened my mouth to tell Mrs. Iwuchukwu that I would drink every bit of the milk in the fridge if she let me leave the table right away. I could hear floorboards creaking from upstairs, which meant Travis and Ben must have finished their showers already, and I couldn't wait anymore.

"OK, then, off you go," said Mrs. Iwuchukwu, and she pushed in her chair so that I could squeeze between her and the kitchen counter.

"Me too!" said Noah, licking the last bit of ketchup from his fingers and jumping down from the table to follow me.

There was a bang at the front door, and Sophie came running down the corridor, her feet like thunder. As she came into the kitchen, she threw her bag on the floor and grunted, "Starving!" Then she gave me a look that seemed to say it was my fault she was hungry.

Telling my cheeks to stay a normal color, I hurried out of the room and ran up the stairs, Noah racing up behind me. I stopped in front of Travis's door, but before I could knock on it, it flew open.

"C-come in," said Travis. His words sounded strange coming out from behind the long stream of shiny brown hair that covered his face like a waterfall. It was all drippy and wet, and small droplets of water were falling everywhere.

Noah pushed into the room before me and immediately ran for the superhero models on Travis's bookshelves.

"Be c-careful," said Travis, quickly putting some of the bigger models out of Noah's reach. "You c-can play with thish one," he offered, giving Noah a model of Batman. "And th-thish one," he added, holding out one of the Incredible Hulk.

Noah nodded seriously and grasped them in his hands like lollipops that he couldn't wait to start licking.

"Where's Ben?" I asked as Travis shut the door.

"S-still getting changed," Travis said with a shrug, staring at me for exactly seven seconds without blinking.

"Look," he said, turning around, picking up his rucksack, and pulling out a newspaper. "It'sh your, er, st-star."

I looked down and felt Noah run to my side. There, taking up the whole front page, was the same picture we had seen last night, of Mum's burning star going up, up, up through a black sky of space. And above it, in giant letters, were the words:

OUR NEW ROCK STAR!

I took the paper and held it straight so that Noah and me could look at the picture properly. It felt like a rocket was lifting off inside me. Mum wasn't just a star! She was a rock star! A real live rock star! I wanted to hug the paper and hold it for at least a thousand years. Maybe I would have if Travis wasn't there, but he was, so instead I gave him a smile and said, "Thanks."

"Niyah? Is that really Mum?" asked Noah, moving his face so close to the paper that his nose touched the page.

I nodded, and he suddenly lunged forward and gave the picture of Mum's star a giant "Mwah!" I had nearly forgotten the sound of it, but it was the same kiss he used to give Mum when she was dropping us off at school.

"Y-you can keep that," said Travis, looking proud. I stared down at the paper, wanting to read every single thing it was saying about Mum right away. But I wanted to read it on my own—so that I could look at the pictures extra closely and drink in all the words, like a delicious peanut butter milk shake. I forced my eyes to look away from it, and gave Travis a nod.

"I got it f-from my t-teacher at school." Travis grinned. "A-and Ben and me got thish for you. . . ."

Turning around, Travis looked through his rucksack again and took out a book.

"We t-took it from the library—from our s-school's tripsh shelf," explained Travis. "Our class went last year, but we haven't b-been—b-because we came t-too late."

I gave the newspaper to Noah and told him to be extra careful with it. Then I took the shiny book Travis was holding out to me. In one corner it said *Souvenir Guide* in fat white letters, and in the middle of the page was the photograph of a tall red-bricked building. It had small round lights going all the way around it—just like the round lights on a ship—and instead of a normal pointy roof, it had a large gray domed one that looked like a giant onion someone had cut in half and then taken a slice out of. Pointing out from the middle where the missing slice was, was a large white telescope.

I quickly flicked through the pages. There were lots of old pictures of strange-looking machines and giant telescopes, colored pictures of golden clocks, maps that looked like globes, and paintings of old men from history pointing out of windows. It was one of the best, most exciting books I had ever seen.

"And l-look here!" said Travis.

Taking the book from me, he flicked right to the back. There, across two pages, was a map called "A Map of Greenwich in London." It showed a bright blue, bendy river labeled THE RIVER THAMES with cartoon buildings all around it. There was Buckingham Palace and Big Ben and St. Paul's Cathedral, which were all buildings I had been to before on trips with Mum. And a strange building that looked like a bullet, called "the Gherkin," which I had never seen. They were all squished together on one side of the river. And on the other side was the London

Eye—which looked like a Ferris wheel but which I knew wasn't one really. Next to the wheel were lots of trees, and then a ship that looked like an old pirate ship with lots of sails, named the *Cutty Sark;* a flat-roofed building that looked like a small castle, called the Queen's House; and a big building called the National Maritime Museum. And behind all of them, in the middle of a big patch of green, was the picture of a domed building with a telescope poking out labeled ROYAL OBSERVATORY GREENWICH.

"That's where we n-need to go," said Travis, pointing to the telescope.

"Yeah!" said Ben, making me and Travis jump. "What?" he asked, looking at us as if he had always been there, and patting his hair. It was wet too, but because his hair was so fluffy, all the small balls of water didn't drip or fall down at all. They stayed where they were, like extra-shiny bubbles that were waiting to be popped. He was wearing his Newcastle hoodie the wrong way around again, but this time, instead of eating biscuits from the hood, he was eating a large bag of crisps.

Looking at the map again, I tried to find the words *Waverley Village* on it. But I couldn't see any villages on it at all.

"Where are we on here?" I asked, handing the map over to Travis so that he could show me.

But Travis shook his head. "We're not on this m-map. It'sh only of L-London."

"Can we get a better map on your computer?" I asked Travis. "Could it show us how to get from here to the star hunters?"

"Let'sh shee!" said Travis, going to his computer and switching it on. Ben and me stood around his chair and waited, because we knew the computer would have the answer. Computers always had the answer to everything, and whatever they said was nearly always true. That's why I had to get to the star hunters before their computers picked a new name for Mum's star. If I didn't get to them in time, everyone would believe the computers and not me.

"What are you looking at?" asked Noah. Leaving the newspaper but still gripping Travis's toys in his hands, he came and joined us. Noah loves computers. At home, he always got into trouble for trying to play on Dad's computer, even though it was a golden rule that we weren't ever allowed to touch it. If we did, Dad's switch would flick on straightaway. But sometimes Noah forgot.

Ben opened up a map web page, then typed in the name of the village we were in, and then *Royal Observatory Greenwich* in a box that said *Your Destination*. Instantly, different-colored lines popped up on the map. The first one had a picture of a car above it and *2 hours 34 minutes* next to it. The second one had a picture of a train next to it and said *1 hour 54 minutes.* The third one had a walking stick figure next to it and *1 day* beside it. But the most important one, the one with a little bicycle on top, said *6 hours 30 minutes.* I felt my mouth drop open. I had never been on a six-hour bike ride before.

"Whoa, it's a whole day to walk there!" said Ben. "That's stupid far."

"Where are we going?" asked Noah, looking at the map and then at me.

Shaking my head at him to tell him that he wasn't coming with me, I got ready to tell Ben and Travis my plan.

"I—I'm not going by train—or bus—or by walking," I said. "I'm going to go by . . . bike!"

"Bike?" Travis looked up at me.

I nodded. "That's if—if you'll let me borrow one of yours?"

Ben and Travis looked at each other for a moment and then at me. And then at the exact same time, they grinned.

"That's what we thought too," said Ben. "That it'd be easiest on our bikes! And you can take Sophie's. Mrs. I. will let us stay out late for Halloween too!"

"Yeah," said Travis. "And if we all leave for t-trick-or-treating early, we c-can get a head start before Mrs. I. even kn-knowsh where we are!"

"Yeah! She might kill us when she finds out we're in London, but then, when we tell her it was for your mum, she'll understand," said Ben, giving me an encouraging punch on the arm.

I looked up at Ben and Travis, feeling surprised. With all the excitement of finding Mum's star, I had forgotten it was going to be Halloween tomorrow.

"Wait! What about if we tell Mrs. I. we're going to go round Dan's after trick-or-treating too?" asked Ben. "So that she thinks we're staying out for longer?"

"And we c-can say we need our b-bikes to get to Dan'sh!" added Travis.

"Yeah." Ben grinned. "He can cover for us! So all we need is a good map. And some flashlights!"

"W-we?" I asked, looking at them confused.

"Yeah," said Travis. "You can't g-go on your own! You'll get losht."

"Or kidnapped," said Ben, stuffing another huge handful of crisps into his mouth. "There's *loads* of kidnappers looking for kids on bikes at nighttime! It's on the news all the time."

"No it's not," I said, frowning. Dad was always watching the news to see if the hedges his bank looked after were OK, and I had never heard of anyone being kidnapped on a bike in the middle of the night.

"Niyah! Where we *going*?" asked Noah, pulling on my arm and getting louder.

I was too surprised by what Ben and Travis had said to answer Noah. They had made a plan too . . . even though it was Mum's star, and it was *my* job to make sure it was named after her. Not theirs. My plan didn't include Ben and Travis. It didn't include anyone else at all! Not even Noah—he was too small anyway.

"You don't have to come," I said. "It's *my* mum's star."

"And mine!" said Noah, starting to look cross.

"But we can help," said Ben.

"Yeah," said Travis as he put his finger to the screen and followed the bicycle line all the way down until it stopped at the Royal Observatory. "S-six and a half hours!" he said. "You don't want to be alone for that l-long in the dark!"

"Where are you going for six and a half hours, Ani-yah?" asked Noah, pulling on my arm even harder.

"Yeah. That's gonna be a looooooooong night," said Ben, nervously stuffing another handful of crisps into his mouth.

"The c-competition finishes at m-midnight tomorrow." Travis quickly stuck out his fingers one by one like the wooden sticks on a hand fan being opened. "So we've got less than t-twenty-two hours—if we t-take away the time we need to g-get there. And half an hour in c-case we get t-tired and need a b-break. . . ."

"That's less than a day." Ben started chomping even louder on his crisps. "When should we leave?"

"You won't need to leave!" I said, my voice getting louder. "I can do this on my own!"

Ben and Travis fell quiet as both of their pairs of eyes got wider and rounder.

"It's my job to make sure Mum's star gets the right name. Not yours! I never said I wanted you to come."

"Oh," said Travis, suddenly turning red and looking down at the floor so that his hair covered his face again. "S-sorry," he mumbled, immediately making me feel bad.

"We just—we just wanted to help," said Ben, shrugging and looking embarrassed. "But we won't . . . if—if you don't want us to."

"I want to see Mum's star!" said Noah, looking around at us as if he finally understood what we were talking about. "Niyah, can I go?" he asked, staring at me with a confused face.

I stayed silent and looked down at my hands. They were clenched into tight fists and I could feel my heart beating inside them. I wanted to tell the star hunters all about Mum on my own—because she was my mum, and I hadn't been with her when she left us. Maybe if I had, she would never have disappeared. But if I could get her name right and make sure everyone in the world knew who she was, then I could make her proud. Just like she had made me feel proud when I had seen her picture in the newspaper. . . .

I looked over at the newspaper lying on Travis's bed next to the souvenir guide and suddenly felt ashamed. Ben and Travis only wanted to help, and I wouldn't have even known about how to get to the star hunters, or that Mum was famous now, if it hadn't been for them. Maybe I wasn't meant to help Mum on my own. Star hunters always needed a team to help them find new stars, so maybe they were meant to be my team too. . . .

"Sorry," I said quietly. "You can come. You too, Noah."

Noah grabbed my hand and hugged it before jumping off the chair to play with Travis's toys again.

"You sure?" asked Ben, frowning so hard it looked as if his forehead was stuck.

I nodded. "As long as it doesn't get you into too much trouble and stop you from being adopted."

"Nah!" said Ben. "Mrs. I. will get mad, but then she'll be OK when she knows it was for your mum and that we weren't running away or anything."

"Sho Noah's c-coming too?" asked Travis, frowning. "Won't he get t-too tired?"

"I'm not tired!" Noah said, giving Travis a push. I knew Noah coming would make the plan harder, but I also knew Mum wouldn't like me leaving him behind on an adventure that had to do with her. She had said it was my job to make sure he wasn't ever scared, and I knew that if he woke up in the middle of the night and found out I wasn't next to him anymore, he would be more scared than even I could imagine.

"Don't worry, I'll look after him," I promised. "He can ride on the bike with me."

"OK." Travis shrugged. "We can t-take it in t-turnsh if you get tired." Turning around in his chair, he looked back at the computer screen. "We n-need to get there by midnight. That m-means we need to leave before . . ." He paused to count on his fingers. "Before five-thirty t-tomorrow afternoon. And we need to get l-lots of things r-ready before then."

"But how are we going to leave by five-thirty?" I asked. "Will Mrs. Iwuchukwu let us go trick-or-treating by then?"

Ben shook his head. "She said me and Travis can go at six. That was last week—before you came here. Maybe we can ask her to let us leave a bit earlier. But we *have* to make sure she lets you both come with us too."

"Why?" I asked. "Won't she let us?"

Ben shrugged as Travis said, "You're n-new. Sho she might th-think you won't like it."

"Yeah, so tonight you *have* to make it seem like you reeeeeeeally want to go trick-or-treating with us!" said Ben.

I nodded.

"So we need to g-get our bikes and Sophie's f-from the shed . . ."

"And some snacks for the journey," added Ben. "Last time I ran away, I went back because I got hungry."

"You've run away before?" I asked, staring at Ben.

"Yeah! *Loads* of times," said Ben. "But not from here. From my last foster house. They weren't that nice to me, so I ran away. That's why I got sent here."

I didn't know what to say, because I couldn't imagine anyone wanting to be horrible to Ben. Instead I nodded, as if I had run away lots of times too.

"And f-flashlights! And we need to g-get the map p-printed— Wait!" Travis opened up a drawer, took out an exercise book, and ripped out a piece of paper from its middle. "Let'sh write it d-down!" As Travis began to write out a plan, Noah grabbed a pen and began drawing pictures on the side of the piece of paper from all the words he was hearing us say.

"What shall we call it?" asked Ben, looking down at it proudly when we were all finished.

Travis looked at me as Noah made one last drawing on the bottom corner of the paper. His tongue was sticking out, which meant he was concentrating really hard, and when it was finished, we could see it was a messy star that looked like it might also be a Christmas tree.

"The Star Hunters' Top-Secret Mission," I said, listening to my words to make sure they sounded right.

"Or! What about 'The Star Hunters' *Midnight* Mission'?" suggested Ben. "'Cause we have to get to the observatory by midnight."

"How about . . ." Travis wrote something at the top of the list and showed it to us, which made us all nod. The plan was perfect now, so we all stayed quiet and read it through again:

The Star Hunters' Top-Secret Midnight Mission!

1. Print out the map—without Mrs. I. seeing!!!
(Do it when Mrs. I.'s making breakfast!)
(Ben switch the printer on in Mrs. I.'s office and wait for me—Travis—to press Print from my computer!)
(Aniyah stay outside the office and make bird noises if anyone comes.)
(Aniyah practice bird noises tonight!)
2. Make Mrs. I. let Aniyah and Noah come trick-or-treating.

3. Find flashlights!

(Probably in shed. But make sure they've all got batteries.)

4. Hide things from breakfast and lunch and tea so we can eat them in the night.

5. Wear warm clothes under Halloween costume (but not too warm).

6. Ben and me to get our allowance money for emergencies.

7. Get all three bikes from shed and tell Mrs. I. we want to go to Dan's after.

8. Pretend to go trick-or-treating but not really go.

9. Follow the map to get to the observatory.

10. Stop the star hunters from naming Aniyah's mum's star wrong!

"So . . . ," said Ben as we all stood and nodded at the plan. Even Noah was quiet and serious.

I thought it was the most perfect plan ever. But a question was poking my mind.

"Why . . . why are you both helping me so much?" I asked, frowning at Ben and Travis. Usually only really best friends would help you go on a bike ride so far away that you might all get into trouble forever, and we had met only a few days ago.

Ben shrugged. "Because we're foster kids, and foster kids stick together no matter what. That's the law."

"Yeah," said Travis quietly. He looked at me and then Noah and added, "And because we're like b-brothers and sistersh now, yeah?" He stared at me for three seconds, then finished with a grin.

I stared back. I had never thought anyone could have a brother or a sister that they hadn't grown up with or whose parents weren't your parents. But I liked the idea of having more brothers. And of Noah having more brothers to look after him too. Just in case anything ever happened to me and I had to disappear like Mum did.

"Plus, you've *got* to help someone if they're looking for their mum," said Ben. "Even when they're, you know, not like, really on the earth anymore."

"Kiiiiiiiiiiiiiiiiiiiiiiiiids!" shouted Mrs. Iwuchukwu from downstairs. *"Come and get your hot choco-laaaaaaaaaaaaaaaaaaaates!"*

"Wicked!" said Ben as Travis quickly put the plan into the top drawer of his table and slammed it shut.

I ran back to mine and Noah's room and hid the newspaper and the souvenir guide under the bunk bed. And feeling more excited than I had ever felt before in my whole entire life—even more excited than when Mum and Dad had taken me and Noah to Disneyland for Christmas last year—I quickly followed Ben, Travis, and Noah down the stairs, wishing that tomorrow night was already here.

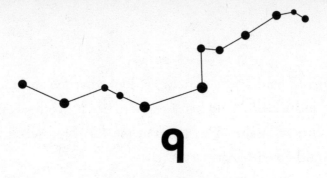

9

The Shape-Shifter

The next morning, I woke up clutching my locket and feeling so happy that, at first, I couldn't remember where I was. But after a few seconds, my brain woke up and made me sit up so fast I banged my head on the top bunk. Today was Saturday—it was Halloween. And the day the Star Hunters' Top-Secret Midnight Mission was going to happen! By this time tomorrow, the royal star hunters would know Mum's real name, close the competition, and tell the world what her star was really called. Even Dad might hear about it and know what me and Noah had done, and come and find us too!

I jumped out of bed and ran over to the window. The sun was up, but I could tell it was still really early because the grass was covered by a white mist that moved like ghosts going for a walk. I didn't know how long I would have to wait in the bedroom until Mrs. Iwuchukwu came to get us, because this was our first Saturday in her house. At home, Mum always woke us up half an hour later on weekend days, so maybe it was the same here. But I was too excited to go back to sleep, so I got my star map from the front pocket of my rucksack, and the newspaper and the souvenir guide out from under the bunk bed, and went to sit by the window.

Even though I had read all about Mum being a rock star to Noah before Mrs. Iwuchukwu had come to turn off the lights last night, I wanted to read it again all by myself. So that's what I did. Three whole times. I wanted to remember every single sentence—like the one that said Mum had "stumped the greatest astronomers in the world" and "broken the very foundation of physics." And the other one that said she was "making history with every passing second."

But the best thing about the paper wasn't the words. It was being able to touch the picture, and know that it was real. When Mum had made us run away to hide in the hotel-that-wasn't-really-a-hotel, she had forgotten to pack any of our photographs from home. She only had one photograph of me and Noah and her together, and it had been inside her purse. But I didn't know where that was anymore or if I would ever see it again, so the newspaper was the only photo I had of Mum now. The rocket ship inside me came alive when I touched it, and I promised myself that I would keep the picture safe until I could grow up and put it in a frame for all of time. It made me wonder if the royal star hunters would let me see Mum as a star in the sky through their extra-powerful telescope too—right up close! I told my brain to remember to ask, because I was sure they would let me.

After I looked just as hard as I could at Mum's star so that my brain couldn't ever forget what it looked like, I folded the paper up, put it next to me, and opened up the souvenir guide. I had to learn as much as I could about the observatory so that when the royal star hunters met me, they would know that it was OK to let me use the telescope to see Mum and that I wouldn't break it. But the guide was much harder to read than I thought it was going to be. It wasn't like any of the souvenir guides we got at Disneyland or the zoo. It was more like a science textbook from school and had lots of words in it that I had never heard of before, like *octant* and *altazimuth* and *zenith*—which all sounded like weapons that superheroes might use to beat up their enemies.

I flipped through the pages until I came to a black-and-white picture of lots of women waving. The writing next to it said that the royal star hunters didn't use just their compasses to measure the stars, but human computers too! I had never heard of human computers before, but it made me think that Travis could be ours, because he seemed to like numbers and did math on his fingers all the time. But then the next line said that all the royal human computers were always women, so I guessed I would have to be it instead—even though I still got my seven and my eight times tables mixed up.

I closed the guide and opened up my star map. I had to tell Mum to stop near one of the constellations that were close to me and Noah. Crossing my fingers and closing my eyes tight, I told Mum just as loud as I could inside my head that she had to land somewhere outside Mrs. Iwuchukwu's second-floor window—the one at the back of the house, not the front. Then I told all the other stars to please help her to know where to stop too. I didn't know if stars could speak or if they used a special sign language made up of flashes and winks. But I was sure they could understand English. Dad always said that everyone in the whole galaxy knew some English.

"Rise and shine!" cried out Mrs. Iwuchukwu as the bedroom door swung open. I quickly jumped up and hid everything behind my back. I had been too busy shouting at the stars inside my head to hear anything outside it.

"Ah! You're up, Aniyah! Good girl." Mrs. Iwuchukwu

smiled as she began to sniff the air. She had silver glitter on her eyes today to match her gray dress and had big, gray, feathery earrings in her ears. I thought she looked like a gray parrot I had seen in London Zoo once. Only nicer.

"Go and get cleaned up, please," she said, "while I see if Noah has left me a present, eh?"

I nodded as Noah sat up in bed, rubbing his eyes. This was it! Time to start the Top-Secret Midnight Mission!

After brushing my teeth super fast, I quickly got dressed and waited for Mrs. Iwuchukwu to take Noah for a shower, just like she always did after she had cleaned the bed. But instead of going downstairs to wait for breakfast like usual, I crept up to Travis's door and did the super-secret knock he had taught me last night—which was two slow knocks followed by three quick ones.

Ben opened the door and pulled me in.

"Ready?" he asked, looking excited. He was wearing a football T-shirt with his name on it and black shorts and bright red knee-high socks, and Travis looked like he was wearing some extra-shiny white pajamas—except they were much cooler because they weren't pajamas at all, but a karate suit.

I nodded as Travis turned his computer on. "But I can't make bird noises," I told them. "I tried all last night, and all I can do is a cuckoo-clock noise or a pigeon."

"A pigeon?" asked Ben, frowning.

I nodded and gave a "Cooooo . . . coooooo . . . !" to show him.

"That just sounds like a cuckoo," said Ben. "Only slower."

"It's not. It's different. But that's why a cat noise is better," I explained. I made a *meeeeeoooooow* sound, then said, "See?"

"OK." Ben shrugged. "We'll do cat noises, then."

"It'sh l-long," said Travis, shaking his head and scrolling down the computer screen. He had opened up the bike map we had looked at yesterday and was reading the instructions. "It'sh sheven p-pages!" he said as he reached the last sentence that said *Your Destination—Royal Observatory Greenwich.*

We all stared at the screen nervously.

Suddenly, I heard a creak outside the door and turned around. Ben and Travis heard it too, but the door stayed closed and everything became silent again, so we turned back around to the computer screen.

"Sho, Aniyah—you d-do the cat signal for me as soon as Ben'sh turned on the p-printer, yeah?" said Travis. "And then p-pretend you're doing s-something but not really," he instructed.

"Shhhh!" said Ben suddenly, sticking out his hands and staying still.

We all fell silent and listened extra hard. There was lots of thumping on the stairs, and after a few seconds, we could hear the radio being switched on and Mrs. Iwuchukwu getting things out from the fridge and Noah banging on the kitchen table.

"C-come on!" said Travis as he grabbed his computer mouse and hovered the arrow over the picture of a printer. "She'sh in the kitchen already!"

"Ready?" asked Ben, looking at me with the most serious face I had seen him use.

I nodded, even though my insides were all jumping up and down like extra-bouncy frogs.

"Come on, then," said Ben, touching his hair on the sides like he was getting ready to go to a fashion show and not downstairs to secretly turn on Mrs. Iwuchukwu's printer.

I followed Ben out of Travis's room and copied him as he tiptoed along the corridor and down the creaking stairs. Coming to a stop at the edge of the kitchen door, he looked over his shoulder at me and put a finger to his lips, then peeked around the corner. I was worried Mrs. Iwuchukwu would see his hair before he could see anything at all, but then, like a ballet dancer dressed in football shorts, he leaped past the kitchen doorway and landed on the other side. Hearing the sink turn on, I gulped and leaped too, but landed on Ben's toes.

"Ouch!" whispered Ben, rubbing his toes with his hands.

"Sorry!" I whispered back.

Rolling his eyes, Ben waved me on and, using his socks to slide up the wooden floor of the corridor, stopped outside Mrs. Iwuchukwu's office door.

Ben grabbed the doorknob and twisted it until it clicked open. "Thank God Mrs. I. never locks it," he whispered. "I'm going in—wait for a meow from me!" he added before disappearing through the gap in the doorway like a shadow and closing the door behind him.

"*Aniyaaaaaaaauaaaaaaaaaah!*" cried out Mrs. Iwuchukwu from the kitchen, making me jump. "*Bennnnnnnn! Trrrrrraaaaaaaavisssssssss! Sophieeeeeeeeeeeeeee! Breakfast now, please!*"

From inside the office, I heard a "Meow! Meow!" and sprang into action. I ran past the kitchen door so quickly that I knew Mrs. Iwuchukwu wouldn't be able to see me, then skidded to the bottom of the stairs and gave a loud "Meeeeeeeeeeeeooooooooooooooooow! Meeeeeeeeeeeeeeooooooooooooow!" hoping Travis could hear me above the radio music but that Mrs. Iwuchukwu and Sophie couldn't hear me at all. Then I tiptoed back past the kitchen. Luckily Mrs. Iwuchukwu was too busy banging on the toaster to see me.

I waited as still as a metal statue in a park for something to go wrong. But the radio music kept on playing, and I could hear Mrs. Iwuchukwu telling Noah to sit down properly. There was no noise on the staircase, which meant it was still empty and Sophie was still upstairs.

Pressing my ear to the office door, I held my breath and crossed my fingers and concentrated hard. *Please let the map print out! Please let the map print out! Please let the map print out.*

After a few seconds, I heard a machine coming to life and then Ben calling out, "Meow!"

It was working! The printer was printing! Now all I had to do was go into the kitchen and keep Mrs. Iwuchukwu busy until Ben and Travis had finished—just like we had planned.

I stood up straight and turned around, ready to run into the kitchen. But instead I found my face bumping into a wall of silver sequins. My eyes traveled up and reached Sophie's. She was standing in front of me with a smile on her face and her arms crossed, as if she had been watching me the whole time. I instantly felt like something heavy had fallen off a shelf inside my stomach and landed next to my feet.

"What do we have here, then?" she asked, looking over my shoulder as if she had X-ray vision and could see through the door. "Stealing something, are we?"

I shook my head and opened my mouth, hoping it could give a warning meow to Ben. But my voice had turned chicken and was hiding somewhere behind my tonsils, and nothing came out at all. So I waited for Sophie to do something. Maybe she was going to push past me and catch Ben and take our map from the printer and ruin everything. Or maybe she was going to call Mrs. Iwuchukwu and tell her I was a thief and that the police needed to come right away!

But Sophie didn't do either of those things. Instead she smiled and said, "Don't worry . . . I won't tell!" and gave me a wink.

It was the first wink Sophie had ever given me, and it made me smile back and feel worried at the same time.

"Thank you?" I said, even though the voice that said it didn't sound like mine at all.

Sophie gave a nod. But then, in the very next moment, her smile disappeared, and her lips and eyes became as thin as each other. Then suddenly she said, "Not unless I really want to!" turned around, and ran off into the kitchen shouting, *"Mum! Aniyah's trying to steal from your office! I've just seen her!"*

From behind the office door I could hear a sudden thump, and from the floorboards upstairs I could hear running feet and from inside my ears I could hear someone beating a drum. And I knew right away that they were all the sounds of a top-secret mission that had gone horribly wrong.

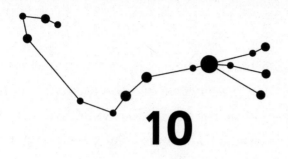

10

The Lost Day

When I saw both Mrs. Iwuchukwu and Sophie hurrying out of the kitchen, I knew instantly what I had to do: I had to make a distraction! I used to make them all the time at home when I wanted to help keep Dad away from Mum and Noah. But I didn't know what kind of distraction would work with Mrs. Iwuchukwu, so I had to guess. I wished I could pretend-cry, but I couldn't. Instead, I stood up straight and waited, listening as Noah jumped down from the kitchen table to have a look and Travis hurried down the stairs.

"Aniyah? What's going on here?" asked Mrs. Iwu-chukwu as she came and stood in front of me with her eyebrows raised. She didn't look as angry as she had done when the bowl of spaghetti had smashed onto the floor. She just looked confused.

Forcing my mouth to open, I began my distraction.

"*Please, Mrs. Iwuchukwu! It's all my fault!*" I said, as loudly as I could so that Ben could hear me and make the printer finish faster. I hadn't heard him meow again, so the map had to still be printing!

"*It was my idea! I made a dare to see what was behind the door—and Ben said I should just ask you. But then I dared him to go in first and he said OK and then he did. But that's all! We weren't stealing anything, I promise!*"

Mrs. Iwuchukwu's frown changed from being one line to being three squiggly ones.

Sophie shook her head. "No! Mum! She's lying!" she said. I watched as she opened her mouth again, but before she could say anything else, I opened mine first. I had to keep my distraction going for as long as I could, even if I didn't know what I was going to say.

"*It's true!*" I shouted, feeling my cheeks and the end of my nose becoming hot. "We *weren't* stealing anything! *I promise! I made the dare!* And Travis said I shouldn't, but I did it anyway. It's my fault and . . . you can punish me if you like. . . ." My voice became quieter until it vanished into silence.

"It'sh t-true, Mrs. I.!" said Travis, his eyes almost popping out of his head.

Mrs. Iwuchukwu nodded and, telling me to stand aside,

116

reached for the doorknob. A large bubbling stingray began to rise at the back of my throat. I knew Mrs. Iwuchukwu was going find the printer printing and Ben meowing and the top-secret mission everywhere . . . which meant Noah and me were going to be taken away by the police and I was definitely going to be sick all over the floor.

The door swung open and Mrs. Iwuchukwu stepped inside as me and Sophie and Noah and Travis all pushed in behind her. My eyes felt as if they were full of heartbeats as I blinked hard inside the much darker room. After two seconds, I saw blinds at a large window and Ben sitting in Mrs. Iwuchukwu's office chair, spinning around on it as if he was trying to make himself dizzy. As soon as he saw us, he jumped up as if he was surprised.

"Sorry, Mrs. I.!" he said, trying to stand up straight.

Mrs. Iwuchukwu said, "Hm!" and walked in, looking around. I saw Travis glance over at a large black printer that sat on top of a tall block of metal drawers. I looked at it too—but it was switched off, and there weren't any papers on its little shelf.

"Right," said Mrs. Iwuchukwu, walking over to the metal drawers and pulling on them to make sure they were locked. "Well, nothing out of place here. . . . Now, everyone out! Breakfast is getting cold and we're running late already! And, Aniyah?"

I stopped and waited for Mrs. Iwuchukwu to start shouting at me. But instead she said, "Next time you want to see anything, all you have to do is ask, darling. I'm not hiding anything, and this is your house too. OK?"

I nodded, even though I didn't believe her. People who didn't have anything to hide didn't have locked drawers. And Mrs. Iwuchukwu had three of them.

"But, *Mum*! They're *lying*!" cried Sophie, looking over at Ben suspiciously. "I heard them say they were going to steal something—for—for a dare!"

"Ben, have you stolen anything from this room?" asked Mrs. Iwuchukwu.

Ben shook his head and showed everyone his hands.

"Aniyah, is there anything you want to take—or borrow—from this room?"

I shook my head too.

"Well, there we are, then. Sophie, you must have heard wrong, eh? Come on! Time for breakfast!" Mrs. Iwuchukwu put her hand on Noah's shoulder and, taking the spoon he had been sucking out of his mouth, led him back to the kitchen.

I waited for Sophie to leave too. But she didn't move at all. She stayed exactly where she was and glared at all of us. It was a glare so strong that it made my breath stop. It was like she was trying to hypnotize everyone with her eyes—just like the snake with the swirling eyes in *The Jungle Book* cartoon Mum had let us watch one time. Except that snake was silly and funny, and Sophie wasn't either of those things.

We all waited for her to say something, and I could see Travis and Ben were holding their breaths too.

After a few seconds, Sophie pointed a finger at us. "I don't know exactly what you're up to," she said, her whisper sounding like a hiss. "But I'm going to find out, and then you'll see!" And she swiveled around on her heels and left the room.

"Whizzing wombles!" said Ben, breaking out into a grin and making me and Travis breathe again. "Good thing Mrs. I. didn't come over and check my pants!" Ben jumped up and lifted his football T-shirt. There, pressed against his back and half-tucked into his shorts, were the pages of our map!

"G-good one!" said Travis, giving Ben a high five and smiling so much that all his braces stuck out.

"That's brilliant!" I said, smiling too. I held up both my hands and gave Ben a high ten—just like me and Eddie and Kwan used to do at school.

"Yup, I'm a genius!" Ben nodded. "Maybe that's why my hair is as big as Einstein's! I'll go hide the map in my room after breakfast. . . . Hey! Good job stalling, Aniyah!"

he said, giving me a punch on the arm. "It gave me enough time to get the map into my pants and turn the printer off! You were brilliant."

"Yeah," said Travis, giving me a punch on the arm too. Only his was more of a tap.

"Come on! Who's hungry?" asked Ben. "I could eat about fifteen pieces of toast right now! Special-agent jobs always make me hungry!" And giving us a grin, he half ran and half slid all the way to the kitchen.

After breakfast, I thought Mrs. Iwuchukwu would let everyone go up to their rooms again or play or watch TV together because that's what Mum let us do at home on the weekend most times. But instead, Mrs. Iwuchukwu made us all hurry into the car so that Sophie could go to her drama school and pretend she was an actress, and Ben could play football so badly that he kept getting booed at by his own teammates, and Travis could do karate in a hall with a hundred other karate kids and be shouted at by a very red-faced teacher with bright metal clips in her hair. Then after that it was orchestra rehearsal, where Sophie played the violin and Ben played the cello and Travis sat and stuffed pieces of paper into his ears.

When all the activities were over and we had eaten some sandwiches in the car, we had to go shopping because Mrs. Iwuchukwu needed to get Halloween sweets and bits for everyone's trick-or-treating costumes. That was when Noah made the first part of our plan work without us even having to do anything, because as soon as Mrs. Iwuchukwu went to buy Sophie's witch's hat, he started crying and screaming that he wanted a costume too! He cried so much that in the end Mrs. Iwuchukwu said we could both go out trick-or-treating with Travis and Ben—just so long as we never left them. Ben and Travis gave me a thumbs-up and a wink each, as if I had made Noah cry on purpose. I didn't know how to tell them that I hadn't made Noah do anything at all, so I just gave a thumbs-up back and helped Mrs. Iwuchukwu pick out our costumes.

By the time we finished and finally got home, the kitchen clock said it was past four o'clock. As soon as I saw the time, something small and squiggly began to wriggle around in my stomach. We had less than an hour and a half left until we had to leave—and all we had was the bike map and our costumes! We still had loads left to do. But even after we got home, Mrs. Iwuchukwu still kept us busy. First Ben and Travis had to go and shower because they smelled like socks, and me and Noah had to help put away the shopping. Then we all had to help make dinner because Mrs. Iwuchukwu said nobody was going to be eating bags of sugar on an empty stomach on her watch.

As we all helped in the kitchen, I could feel time

beginning to slip away faster and faster. Travis and Ben still needed to ask Mrs. Iwuchukwu if we could borrow the bikes from the bike shed . . . and we still needed to get all the runaway snacks Ben had secretly made Mrs. Iwuchukwu buy. And get the flashlights! How were we ever going to leave in time?

By the time Ben and Travis had finished their showers and dinner was ready, I was starting to feel as if an entire ocean was moving around inside me. What if Father Time was still angry with me and was making us lose the day on purpose? What if the plan didn't work and Mum's star got stuck with someone else's name? What if I couldn't ever make things right? I could hear the ticks and the tocks of the kitchen clock getting louder and louder, as if it was trying to warn me that time was running away.

Finally, just as I was starting to think that it wasn't really Halloween at all and we weren't ever going to be allowed out, Mrs. Iwuchukwu clapped her hands and said, "Oooh! You better get your costumes on! I can hear them coming already!"

A second later, the doorbell rang as some voices called out, "Trick or treeeeeeat!"

Feeling the blood begin to rush around inside me like a river I couldn't control, I stood up.

Mrs. Iwuchukwu frowned at me for a second before

smiling. "Ah! No need, Aniyah! You finish dinner. I'll take care of them."

"Candice and Roberta are coming to get me at seven, Mum," Sophie said as Mrs. Iwuchukwu jumped up from her chair, quickly grabbed a large bowl of sweets from the kitchen counter, and ran out into the corridor. "I'm not going anywhere with you losers!" added Sophie, giving us an I-hate-all-of-you stare as she left the room too.

I sneaked a look up at the clock while Mrs. Iwuchukwu was out of the room. It was exactly 6:21 p.m. It was so late! And we weren't even ready yet!

"Aniyah!" whispered Ben as soon as we were all alone. "You *have* to say you want to come to Dan's, OK?"

I nodded as Travis gave me a thumbs-up, while Noah licked his plate and nodded.

"And we *have* to get Mrs. I. out of the kitchen somehow so I can get our snack food," said Ben, looking over at all the kitchen cupboards that were holding our treats hostage.

"We'll think of s-something upstairsh," said Travis.

"Mrs. I.! Can we take our bikes—and borrow Sophie's for Aniyah?" asked Ben as soon as Mrs. Iwuchukwu came back. The bowl of sweets in her hand was half-empty, which made me think of Mum. She always gave everyone too many sweets on Halloween too.

"Why do you want the bikes, eh?" Mrs. Iwuchukwu frowned. "I don't want you going too far tonight! Not when it's your first time looking after Aniyah and Noah."

"But Dan said we can go over to his house to do swapsies if we wanted—he's only a three-minute ride away! And he said Aniyah and Noah can come too!" begged Ben. "Pleeeeeeeease!"

Mrs. Iwuchukwu rolled her eyes and looked at me and Noah as if wondering what to do. "Hmmmm . . . ," she said. "Aniyah, Noah, would you like to go?"

I nodded and said, "Yes, please," which made Noah cry out, "Yeah! Yeah! I want to go on a bike!"

"See!" said Ben, starting to talk more quickly. "Because if they come we've got more sweets to swap and Aniyah can make friends with Dan too!"

I looked at Mrs. Iwuchukwu and nodded and made my eyes as big as they could go too. *Please, please, pleeeeeeease, Mrs. Iwuchukwu, please let us have the bikes,* I whispered inside my head and with my eyes.

"Hmmm," said Mrs. Iwuchukwu, shaking her head at herself. "OK. You can go to Dan's, but you can *walk* there. The bikes are too big for Noah to sit on and I don't want any accidents. But! I'll let you stay out until eight-thirty, so you have time to walk there and back again without rushing, OK?"

Ben and Travis nodded as me and Noah watched to see if they were going to try again. But they didn't. Instead, Ben jumped up and, flinging his arms around Mrs. Iwuchukwu's waist, gave her a hug. "Thanks, Mrs. I.! You're the *best*!" he said, making Mrs. Iwuchukwu shake her head again. I watched as she laughed and then hugged him back, and missed my mum even more than I ever thought I could.

"Off you go," she said, giving us all a smile as she pulled Ben away from her. "Go get ready before it gets too late!"

Nodding, Ben and me and Travis and Noah left the kitchen table to go and put our costumes on. As I reached the kitchen door, I looked up at the clock and saw the large hand click into place over the number six. It was half past six already! But I forced myself to believe that it didn't matter. Time might have made us lose the whole day, and Mrs. Iwuchukwu might have made us lose our bikes, and we might be an hour later than the plan had said, but nothing was going to stop me from getting to the star hunters and making them name Mum's star right. Even if that meant making everyone else—even Noah—stay behind.

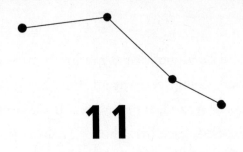

11

The Tiger, the Wardrobe, and the Witch

"It's OK if you don't want to come anymore," I said as we reached the corridor outside our rooms. "Just show me the way a little bit and then I'll go on my own."

"What are you talking about?" asked Ben, frowning at me as he put one hand on the handle of his bedroom door.

"Mrs. Iwuchukwu said we can't have the bikes, remember?" I said, wondering if he'd already forgotten. "And it's too far for us to walk! Especially Noah. So it's better I go on my own."

Ben tutted and shook his head as Travis's frown got deeper.

"Don't be stupid, Aniyah," said Ben.

"Yeah," said Travis. "We're shtill taking the bikesh!"

"We are?" I asked as Noah jumped up and down excitedly.

"Yeah! Of course we are! Mrs. I. said we can't ride

them to Dan's—so we won't. We'll just ride them to London instead! See?" Ben's eyebrows jumped up and down at me as Travis nodded. "*Technically,* we're not *not* doing what she said."

"Oh," I said, suddenly feeling so happy I wanted to hug everyone. But instead I just nodded and said, "OK."

"Let'sh hurry and g-get changed and then go!" said Travis, giving us a thumbs-up before he slid behind his bedroom door.

Running back into our room, I saw that Mrs. Iwuchukwu had laid our Halloween costumes out on the bottom bunk bed for us. As soon as Noah saw his, he ran over to it and pulled it on straight over his head. In a few seconds, he had disappeared under a long white sheet to become a ghost—but he had put it on the wrong way around so that the holes for the eyes and the big smile were at the back of his head. I stopped him from running into the bunk bed ladder and twisted the sheet around so that he could see properly.

"Niyah! I'm a ghost!" he said as he began waving his arms up and down happily and making the sheet float around behind them. "Now all the ghosts that live here can be scared of *me*!"

"Yup!" I said as I quickly pulled my bright-orange-and-black-striped costume over my clothes and yanked the large, hairy hood over my head. The stripy tail swung between my legs as I zipped my tiger costume up. I had wanted to be a lion, but the shop Mrs. Iwuchukwu had taken us to didn't have any lion costumes. I guess it didn't matter much, since both lions and tigers are big cats that roar and live in the jungle, which means that under their fur they're really both the same. So instead of being Simba from *The Lion King,* I was going to be a Tiger Queen star hunter—which was just as cool.

I hurried over to the wardrobe, gave a roar at myself in the long mirror, and then took out my school rucksack. I packed my new souvenir guide, my star map, and the newspaper with the picture of Mum's star on it. Then, thinking of Noah, I packed an extra pair of trousers in case he wet himself in the middle of the night.

"Noah, look," I said, holding up a pen—Mum had always put an extra one in the front pocket of my rucksack for school. I had forgotten it was there, and as I held it up, I suddenly had an idea. Stepping inside the wardrobe, I pushed away our clothes and wrote her name on the back wall in large letters. Noah jumped into the wardrobe behind me and, giggling, made more ghost noises.

"Here," I said, giving him the pen. "Draw a picture of Mum—quickly. So that everyone can remember her." I pointed to show him where to do it, and in just a few seconds, Noah had drawn a stick Mum with curly hair and a big smile. When he finished, he gave it a wave from underneath his ghost sheet as if the drawing was secretly real. I nodded and wondered if my idea would work. In *The Lion King,* Rafiki the monkey draws a picture of Simba on a tree in fruit juice and does spells to find him. I would have liked for us to have done that for Mum, but we didn't have a tree trunk or magic fruit and I didn't know any spells. Just a wardrobe and a school pen and a wish.

"Come on," I said, jumping out of the wardrobe and switching off the lights. Noah stopped making his ghost noises and followed me out to Ben's door. After a single knock, it swung open, but instead of Ben's face smiling out at us, a super-shiny black mask that looked as if it had jail bars for a nose and large bug eyeballs for eyes stared back at us. We could still tell it was Ben because his perfectly round Afro surrounded the mask, and he had his Newcastle United hoodie the wrong way around underneath the cloak he was wearing.

"Who are you meant to be?" I asked.

From inside the mask, his voice said, "I'll give you a clue!" Then, stretching out a hand and giving his long black cloak a swish with the other, he said in a deep voice, "I am your faaaaaather."

I frowned as Noah shook his ghost head and said, "No you're not!"

"You know! Darth Vader?" asked Ben, his voice back to normal.

I shrugged.

"From *Star Wars*?"

I shrugged again as Ben lifted his mask and gave me a frown. "You mean you've never watched *Star Wars*—even though you like stars?"

I shook my head, which made Ben look at me as if I had just told him the saddest news he had ever heard.

"Don't worry. We'll change that as soon as we get back home!" he said as Travis's bedroom door opened and he came out into the corridor too.

I looked at Travis and tried not to laugh. He was dressed in a glow-in-the-dark skeleton suit that was like a pajama onesie, but he was so tall and skinny that it looked like the suit was actually a real X-ray of his bones. His hood showed what his skull might look like at the back too.

"Noah! You're a cool gh-ghosht!" said Travis as he patted Noah on the head. Noah's ghost head nodded and his hands tried to give a thumbs-up from underneath the sheet.

"Guys, wait a minute," said Ben, waving us into his room. "I've still got to pack my bag."

Shuffling into his room, we all watched as he ran over

to his bed and fell to his knees. As he searched for something he had hidden under his mattress, me and Noah took a good look around the room. Ben's room was so different from Travis's room that it felt as if we had walked into a completely different house. The walls were covered with black and white stripes and two gray seahorses standing next to a Newcastle United banner—which made it feel as if we had been swallowed by a zebra and were standing inside its belly. And on top of the stripes were posters of different Newcastle United football players and a singer with sparkly socks standing on his tiptoes.

On a long wall, Ben had a bookcase just like Travis did, but Ben's bookcase was filled with hundreds of CDs and football sticker books and tiny bobbleheads of different football players that moved as if an invisible finger was poking them all the time. And instead of a computer on his desk, Ben had an electronic keyboard, a small stereo, and a toy train set going all the way around it.

Seeing the piano, Noah ran toward it, jumped up on Ben's chair, and began to poke at the black and white keys. It was switched off, so no sound came out, but Noah didn't care. It was funny seeing a small ghost trying to play a silent piano.

"Wait!" said Ben, standing up and looking confused. "I can't find it!"

"C-can't find what?" asked Travis.

"The printout of the map . . . ," said Ben, looking at us with his forehead all crinkly. "I put it under here this morning—right here," he added, pointing to his mattress.

He hurried over to his wardrobe, opened it quickly, and looked hungrily through a mountain of clothes. Then, running back to his desk, he checked the drawers, but they only had his school books in them.

Shaking his head, Travis ran over to the bed and searched the pillows. "W-we need the m-map," he said, starting to look worried.

"Looking for *this,* idiots?"

Everyone jumped, and Noah stopped pretend-playing on the keyboard as we all turned to where the voice had come from.

Holding up the printout of the map as she stood inside the doorway was Sophie. Except she didn't look like Sophie anymore. She was wearing a purple wig with hair that went all the way down her back, a purple velvet witch's hat, and a cloak made of sparkling purple-and-black sequins over a long black velvet dress. Her freckles had been covered with lots of makeup and her cheeks and eyes were covered in a gold-and-white powder. She was wearing black lace fingerless gloves through which long purple nails stuck out, and instead of a cauldron, she was carrying a purse in the shape of cat. She was a witch. But she was the coolest, most purple witch I had ever seen.

"Still hiding things under your mattress like a dimwit, Ben," she said, shaking her head and tutting. "I heard you. Planning your stupid top-secret mission to London last night. If Mum found out, she'd report you to the police and social services before you could say, 'B-b-b-but, Mum!'"

Travis's cheeks flushed a bright red as Sophie glared at him with a sneer. I could feel my eyes get wider as I realized that the creaks outside Travis's room last night hadn't been the floorboards groaning like they always did, but Sophie spying on us.

"You give that back!" I said, surprised that my voice wasn't shaking. Taking a step forward, I held out my hand for the map. "That's mine! And Ben's! And Travis's!"

"And *mine*!" added Noah.

Sophie took a long piece of the purple hair between her fingertips and began to twist it around in her fingers. "Yeah, well, you *stole* this paper and the ink from Mum's printer, and as soon as Mum sees it, she'll know what you were all doing in her office and that you lied to her!"

Ben and Travis looked at each other as Noah jumped down off the chair and, forgetting that no one could see his face, stood half hiding behind my legs. I put an arm around him and tried not to feel guilty. I never wanted to hurt Mrs. Iwuchukwu by lying to her. I just wanted to get to Mum's star in time.

"But I *could* give it back . . . ," she said, raising an eyebrow and looking at her hair as if she was talking to it and not to us. "And I *suppose* I could just *not* tell Mum about everything I've heard . . . only I'd need something in return. Something *big*."

I looked over at Ben and Travis and wondered what they were going to do. I didn't have anything that Sophie could want—the only things the lady in the black suit had let me bring from the hotel-that-wasn't-really-a-hotel was my school rucksack and a black trash bag of undercover clothes.

"OK . . . what do you want for the map *and* to not tell on us?" asked Ben slowly, taking a step forward.

"Hmmm . . . let's see. . . ."

Sophie walked into the room and, putting a long purple nail to her chin, looked around. I could feel Noah's hands gripping my legs even tighter, as if he was afraid we might be happy to give him away.

"Now. What do I want . . . ? What do I *want* . . . ?"

Ben looked over at his collection of bobblehead football players anxiously and edged closer to his shelves as if he wanted to protect them.

"Don't be thick," said Sophie. "Who'd want any of

your dumb things . . . ?" Then, with a smile, she turned and looked at me.

"I think I'll have . . . *that,*" she said, pointing at my chest.

"My—my tiger suit?" I asked. Feeling confused, I looked down at my stripes. Sophie was much taller than me, so my costume wouldn't fit her at all.

"No, dumbo," said Sophie. And leaning forward, she placed her finger on the locket around my neck.

"That!" she said. "I want *that!*"

Before I could stop myself, I shook my head and heard myself say, "No!" and felt my fingers grip my silver locket. Even though it didn't have anything inside it, I never took it off. It was the only thing I still had that Mum and Dad had bought for me together, and I knew I never wanted anyone else to have it or wear it except me.

"If you don't give it to me, I'm going to tell Mum *every-thing* about what I've heard. And she won't just report you to your caseworker and the children's services, she'll call the police and they'll split you and Noah up *forever,*" said Sophie, her face and mouth and teeth and purple-glittered eyes swimming closer and closer to my face as if she was a slow-moving shark. "That's what they do to stupid run-away foster kids—they make them leave and split up and never come back. Ask Ben. He should know!"

I looked over at Ben and waited for him to deny it. But he just stayed silent, looking down at the floor as if a crack had suddenly opened up and he wished he could jump inside it.

Everyone fell silent and I knew Noah was scared, because his breathing was getting louder—like a breeze that had gotten stuck in the branches of a tree and couldn't find a way out.

"You've got three seconds . . . ," warned Sophie. "Or I'm calling Mum. One. Two. Thhhhhrrrr—"

"*No!*" I shouted. "Don't! Here!" And forcing my fingers to listen to me, I made them undo the silver chain from around my neck.

Sophie looked at the locket I was holding out to her and, grabbing it, gave me a smile. She held up the map for a second as if she still might keep it and then threw it at us, making the pages fly out everywhere like large, flat white feathers floating to the ground.

I watched as she put my locket around her neck. I tried to swallow the large ball of fire that was burning in my throat. "Ah, that's better." She smiled, shaking her wig back into place. Then, looking at us, she grinned. "You guys are *so* gonna get busted, and when you do, Mum is never gonna keep any of you! I thought I was going to have to try harder to get rid of you—but you're doing it all for me! Thanks for that!"

And smiling at us as if we had just wished her a happy birthday, she turned around and slammed the door behind her. Without my locket I suddenly felt as if I had lost Mum and Dad all over again.

As soon as she was gone, Ben began to pick up all the pages of our bike map and put them in order again. His face had become as dark as his Darth Vader mask, and his eyes still wouldn't look at mine.

"S-sorry, Aniyah," said Travis quietly as he began to help Ben. "We'll g-get it back for you. . . ."

I shrugged, trying to pretend that the necklace didn't matter to me. "It's OK," I said, telling my cheeks to stop burning. "It's more important to get to London. But are you *sure* she won't still tell on us?" I asked, feeling a little bit sick. Now that we knew Sophie knew everything, nothing felt safe anymore.

Ben nodded. "She definitely can't tell on us now," he said. "She's got your locket, and she'll know we'll tell Mrs. I. on her about it if she tells on us."

"B-but we should g-go quickly anyway," said Travis. "J-jusht in cashe! I've g-got the plan in my b-bag." He pointed to the gym bag on his bed.

"And I've got the map now," said Ben, stuffing it into his Newcastle United rucksack.

"But . . . what about the flashlights?" I asked, pointing at our plan. "How will we see the map without a light? And the snacks?"

"Mrs. I. should have some in the shed," said Ben. "We can get them when we get the bikes. We'll worry about the snacks when we're down there."

"We'll have to go around the b-back and climb over," said Travis, and Ben nodded. I didn't understand what they meant, but before I could ask, Mrs. Iwuchukwu started shouting at us from downstairs.

"Kids! Do you want to go trick-or-treating or not? Chop-chop! It's past seven!"

I gasped and felt a loud thump in my chest as if something invisible had given me a kick.

"Come on, let's go!" I cried, running out of the room and down the stairs, not even waiting for the others to catch up. We could still get there in time—but only if we moved fast.

"There you are!" Mrs. Iwuchukwu clapped as we hurried into the kitchen. "Aw! Don't you all look a picture?" And she whipped a camera out from behind her back and flashed a silver spark into all of our eyes.

"Ah, you've got your bags for the treats," she said,

nodding as she patted Ben's rucksack. "Good! I've phoned Dan's mum and left a message to say you'll be over by eight or so for swapsies. And that you're to leave there by twenty past eight at the latest."

"Er, thanks, Mrs. I.," said Ben. "Erm . . . can we take some snacks with us—and some water?"

Travis nodded, which made me nod too.

"What do you need snacks for, eh? You'll be getting a million sweets tonight!" Mrs. Iwuchukwu laughed.

"Oh yeah!" said Ben, his mask nodding up and down.

"But water is a good idea. Flush out all that sugar!" Mrs. Iwuchukwu opened a cupboard, then held out four bottles of water for us to put in our bags.

"Right," said Mrs. Iwuchukwu as we all headed to the front door. "Have a good time—and *don't* eat so many sweets that you get sick! Noah! Did you hear me?"

Noah nodded from under his sheet.

"Thanks." Travis waved as he led the way out into the front garden, which was now filled with pumpkin lights on long sticks poking out of the grass. I hadn't seen them before, and guessed Mrs. Iwuchukwu must have put them out while we were getting changed.

"Yeah, thanks Mrs. I.!" said Ben.

"Thanks, Mrs. Iwuchukwu," I said as Mrs. Iwuchukwu smiled and gave me a pat on my back. I smiled back, feeling guilty. After tonight, she would probably be too mad to smile at me ever again.

As we headed out of the front garden and through the creaky wooden gate, a group of witches followed by an Egyptian mummy and a zombie rushed past us and made their way to Mrs. Iwuchukwu's door.

"This way!" whispered Ben as he signaled at all of us to follow him. Instead of heading up the road now filled with children and parents and floating sweet wrappers, we turned the corner onto the narrow alleyway that lay between Mrs. Iwuchukwu's house and the house next door. We passed a large row of trash cans and came to a stop outside a bright blue garden gate.

Ben gave it a push, but it was locked. "Travis?" he whispered. He took his mask off and held it out to me.

I took it and watched as Travis bent down and, joining his fingers together, created a step with his hands. Smoothly, as if this was something they did every day, Ben slipped a foot into Travis's cupped hands and was lifted up and over the wall as if he was going up in a lift. In a flash he had disappeared on the other side. Moments later there was a click and a creak and the large garden gate swung open.

"Shhhhh!" whispered Ben as he waved us in. "Look! Mrs. I. is in the kitchen!"

The bright yellow glow of the kitchen light shone out at us from the other side of the garden, a shadowy figure visible through the flower-patterned curtains.

"Now what?" I asked, tiptoeing after Travis.

"Now we wait until Mrs. I. leaves the kitchen," whispered Travis.

"And then we go treating?" asked Noah, louder than he should have.

"Shhhhh!" I warned, putting a hand over where I guessed his mouth was. "Yes! But later! First we need to get the bikes so we can go see Mum's star! OK?"

Nodding, Noah wrapped his ghost arms around Travis's legs and fell silent. From somewhere across the night air, an owl hooted as we all watched the kitchen window and waited for the lights to go out.

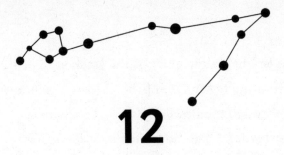

12

The Not-So-Secret Escape

Waiting in the dark, behind a bush, dressed as a tiger, while standing next to a small bored ghost, a glow-in-the-dark skeleton, and a Darth Vader, felt strange. It felt even stranger than the time Dad brought a clown home for Noah as a surprise birthday present. Not a toy clown—a real live human clown who made balloon animals for an hour before disappearing. Dad always liked giving us surprises, and the clown surprise was the funniest, strangest surprise he ever gave any of us. But if he could see me and Noah now, he would definitely think this was stranger!

"Jeepers crackpots, come on!" whispered Ben as the light in the kitchen window continued to shine. "What's taking her so long, anyway?"

"Niyah, I'm bored!" whimpered Noah. "I want to go treating!"

"Shhhhh, Noah, soon! OK? I promise!"

Noah's ghost sighed and leaned against Travis's leg again.

"Look!" said Ben excitedly.

The light in the kitchen window had been switched off.

We held our breaths to see if Mrs. Iwuchukwu would come back again. But she didn't.

"Up there," said Ben, pointing to a window higher up in the house. It had been dark before, but now a light was switched on. "She's gone to her room!"

"OK!" said Travis. "Thish is it!"

We crept over to the garden shed and waited nervously as Travis carefully pulled back the handle of the large silver lock and opened the shed door. At first, all I could see was a dark mass, but after a few seconds my eyes began to understand the shapes they were seeing. I could make out one large bicycle and three smaller ones lying on their sides, as if someone had put them to sleep.

"S-step back!" whispered Travis as he waved us all back out of the shed. "It'll be e-easier if I g-get them out on my own. . . ."

We all stepped back out into the garden as Travis lifted each of the smaller bikes, one by one, and rolled them out into our hands. A few moments later, Ben had a black-and-white-striped bike in his hands, and I had a bright blue one in mine.

Taking his shiny black helmet from the handles, Ben strapped it over his head as I took Sophie's blue helmet and put it on.

"Wait!" whispered Ben as he watched me make the straps on Sophie's helmet shorter. "What about Noah? We haven't got a helmet for him!"

"What about Mrs. Iwuchukwu's?" I asked, pointing back at the shed.

"She hasn't got one," said Ben, shaking his head. "She left it somewhere last year and hasn't bought one since!"

"What'sh wrong?" asked Travis as he shut the shed door and rolled his large red bike over to us.

"We don't have a helmet for Noah," I whispered, feeling like a bad big sister for not having thought of it before.

"Oh," said Travis as we all looked down at Noah. Noah's ghost stared back at us, his wide eyes blinking out through the large droopy holes surrounding them.

"I know!" said Travis. "Wait here!" And he flipped out the kickstand and ran back to the house.

"Where are you going?" whispered Ben, frowning.

But Travis had already reached the kitchen door and slid into the darkness behind it.

For a few seconds, everything felt like a strange dream. From across the night air, a bird began to squawk as a cloud drifted over the moon, plunging the garden into a black hole and making even Noah fall quiet. Ben's mask shone a strange purple black in the moonlight, while Noah's ghost sheet looked like a floating glass of glowing milk.

"Come on," nudged Ben, pushing his mask on top of his hair. "Let's get Noah ready while we wait!"

I nodded, clambering onto Sophie's bike seat as Ben lifted Noah onto the handlebar in front of me.

"Ow! It hurts!" whined Noah as he sat wobbling on the long metal handlebar.

"That's not going to work!" I whispered. "It's the wrong shape!" At home my bike had a low handlebar that made a triangle shape, which Noah could squeeze into whenever he wanted to ride with me. But Sophie's bike wasn't made for sharing.

"What are we going to do?" I asked, feeling panicky.

"Hold on!" Ben whispered back, putting Noah down on the ground again. He tiptoed quickly to the shed and disappeared inside it. A few seconds later, he popped back out, pushing a much bigger bike.

"You can use Mrs. I.'s! And Noah can go in here," whispered Ben, pointing to the big straw basket stuck to the back of the bike. "Don't know why we didn't think of it before!"

"Yipppppeeeee!" cried Noah, which made both me and Ben go, "Shhhhhhhhh!"

"But . . ." I looked from Sophie's bike to Mrs. Iwuchukwu's bike.

"Come on!" urged Ben, reading my thoughts. "We haven't got a choice! As long as you can ride it! And it's not like we're stealing it! We're just borrowing it."

Silently promising Mrs. Iwuchukwu that I would take extra-special care of her bike, I lowered the seat as far as it would go. It was bigger and heavier than Sophie's, and I had to make my legs stretch out more to make the pedals work, but I could just about use my tiptoes to do it. I wrapped my tiger tail around my arm and gave Ben a thumbs-up as he placed Noah in the basket with his legs hanging out over the back of it. It meant Noah would be looking the wrong way and wouldn't see what I was doing, but it would probably be more fun for him anyway.

"Is that OK, Noah?" I whispered, looking down at him over my shoulder.

Noah's ghost sheet nodded and giggled.

"Cool!" said Ben as he quickly wheeled Sophie's bike back to the shed. He had just clicked the lock back into place, when suddenly the most terrifying, deafening crash echoed around our ears.

We all looked back up at the house. The sound of metal tubs tumbling onto the floor like a never-ending row of giant dominoes rang out from the direction of the kitchen, making us all jump with each loud *clang!* Almost instantly, the light in the window next to Mrs. Iwuchukwu's room flashed on, throwing a circle of white onto the shed next to us—as if it had been caught doing something bad by a policeman's flashlight. We waited without breathing, until a second later, the kitchen door flew open and Travis came running out toward us at full speed, carrying what looked like a shiny silver pot with holes tucked under his arm, four bulging trick-or-treat bags crammed in one hand, and something small and square and glowing in the other.

"Ruuuuuuuuuuuun!" he mouthed frantically as another yellow light in the house switched on upstairs.

"Jiminy buckets!" cried out Ben as he ran toward the garden gate trying to wheel both his and Travis's bikes. But before he had taken three steps, Travis whizzed past us and, throwing the treat bags at Ben, grabbed his bike and threw the gate wide open.

"Noah! Sit still and hold on!" I whispered as I pushed the pedals of Mrs. Iwuchukwu's bike just as hard as I could.

I could hear Ben's bike swishing past me and Travis breathing fast as he held the gate open. But no matter how hard I tried, I couldn't make my bike move—it was as if it knew I was trying to steal it and was stopping its wheels from turning!

"The b-brakes!" urged Travis. "Releash the brakes!"

I stared down at my hands and suddenly felt my brain click. Of course! The brakes! My fingers had panicked and were squeezing the brakes! I immediately let go and felt the bike lunge forward as the pedals became free.

"Come on!" urged Ben, pulling down his mask as a light flooded through the kitchen window. Realizing that we were seconds away from being caught, I felt a rush of energy burst out through my feet and, standing up on Mrs. Iwuchukwu's bike, pedaled as hard and as fast as I could. In fewer than two heartbeats, I was through the garden gate feeling the squeal of the wheels beneath me as they landed on the road outside.

"Here!" cried out Travis as he leaned over and stuck a colander upside down on Noah's head before rushing off.

"A space helmet!" cried Noah as the metal holes of the colander slipped down over his eyes.

"That's right!" I replied, quickly turning our bike away from the sounds of someone swimming through a sea of pots and pans and crying out, *"Stop! Thieeeeeeves!"*

Hurtling toward Ben's and Travis's now-disappearing shadows, I rang my bell to let them know I was behind them and, looking back at Noah, warned, "Hold on tight, Noah! We're heading into space!"

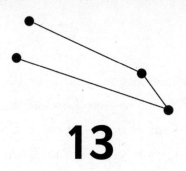

13

The Long Road to Logic Lane

Whizzing down the road, the pedals beneath my feet going faster and faster, I followed Ben and Travis as they zig-zagged between all the trick-or-treaters running around Mrs. Iwuchukwu's street.

"Hey!"

"Watch out!"

"Look, Daddy! A tiger on a bike!"

"Whoa! Slow down!"

"Stupid kids!" cried out different voices as we tinkled our bells and sped by witches and wizards and Franken-stein monsters and at least twelve mini-Draculas carrying bags bursting with sweets. Nearly every house on the street was lit up with bat-shaped fairy lights and pumpkins with plastic candles in them and coffins that popped open when anyone passed by. It all looked like so much fun, and it made me wish that Mum could have been with us, and that instead of having to go to London to see the royal star hunters to tell them all about her, me and Noah could have gone trick-or-treating with her one more time. It would have been nice to feel her holding our hands as we crossed streets and knocked on doors, and to hear her voice telling us to save as many sweets as we could for school. The wish made my throat hurt and my eyes start to go runny, so I pushed it away and tried not to look at all the mums and dads around us who were happy and smiling and together with their families.

Travis followed me but in a few seconds took the lead, speeding off down the street in front of me. "Quick!" he shouted, as if someone was chasing us. At the end of the road he slowed down and, ringing his bell to make sure we all knew what he was doing, turned a corner and disappeared. Ben followed him and swiftly disappeared too, and I swerved hard after them.

"Noah! Are you OK?" I asked, trying to listen for his answer above my heartbeat. Now that I had stolen Mrs. Iwuchukwu's bike on top of running away and making Noah and Travis and Ben run away too, it felt as if my normal heart had been joined by three more.

"Yeeeeeah!" shouted Noah as the bike bumped over

shimmering cobblestones that looked like fish scales made of rock. "This is fuuuuun!" he cried.

Blinking hard so that my eyes didn't lose sight of Ben's and Travis's shadows, I pedaled faster and copied them as they glided left and right and around bendy corners. The road was getting narrower and the trees and bushes all around us seemed to be leaning in closer and closer—as if they wanted to see what we were doing. The night wind rustled the trees' heads and arms and millions of leaves, drowning out the noise of our bike wheels with huge swishes that rose and fell like the waves of an angry ocean, while the moon chased us in between large gray clouds.

I pushed on, trying to feel as happy as I had thought I would feel once we were really on our way to London. But it was hard to feel happy when all my brain could do was wonder how many policemen and caseworkers and women in black suits Mrs. Iwuchukwu was going to send after us. They were probably on their way already. I wondered what was going to happen when they caught us. I guessed that even if I explained everything to everyone and told them I had forced Ben and Travis to help, me and Noah would still get taken away to wherever bad foster kids are taken away to, and split up forever. So that meant that as soon as I fix Mum's name on her star, me and Noah would have to run away for real and try to find Dad so that he could help us. I didn't want to leave Ben and Travis—not when they wanted to be my brothers and were helping me with Mum's star—but it would be better for them if I did. I didn't ever want to do anything that would stop them from getting adopted.

As the streetlights began to fade away and the houses and trees disappeared too, Travis slowed down and, using his bell to warn us not to lose him, turned the sharpest corner yet. Screeching around it, we found ourselves on a narrow lane just big enough for a single car, surrounded by wide-open spaces. I wondered how Travis knew which way to go, because the lane didn't have a road sign and he hadn't stopped to check the bike map even once.

My legs got stiffer as the road began to slant upward, and I saw Ben and Travis slowing too. A long row of bushes that stood to attention like prickly army officers lined the lane, helping us cut through a pitch-black ocean of dry fields lying silent in the dark. The farther and farther we pedaled, the higher and higher the bushes became, until finally, they were so high we couldn't see anything but them and the sky above.

"Hey! Let's . . . sing . . . a song!" panted Ben as he pushed his legs onward with a grunt.

The road was getting even steeper now, and in the dark it looked as if it was turning into a mountain.

"It'll make . . . the time . . . go faster!"

"All right!" shouted Travis, tinkling his bell. "But keep up!"

Telling my legs to keep going, I nodded, trying to think of a song that we all might know.

"Noah—you pick!" cried out Travis. I could feel Noah moving around in the basket as he tried to turn around and see us.

"Careful, Noah!" I warned as the bike wobbled. I couldn't see Noah's face, but he stopped moving. And then suddenly, as if he had been gathering all his energy to shout out his next words, he screeched *"a-wimba-wombaaaaaaaah!"* into the night air.

"A-wimba-what?" asked Ben, swerving on his bike.

I smiled. It was Noah's happy song—the one he always sang to Mum and Dad in the kitchen whenever he knew everyone was feeling happy.

"You know! From . . . *The Lion King* . . . ," I explained, catching up with Ben and cycling right behind him. And feeling glad that it was dark and that he couldn't see how red my face was, I began singing the song at the top of my voice.

"Oh yeah!" said Ben, shining his face into mine. "I know . . . that one!"

From in front of us, Travis sang, "A weeeeeeee-zabimba-imba-waaaaaaaaaay!" Hearing him made Noah so happy that he half jumped up from the basket, crying, *"A-weema-weh, a-weema-weh!"* in return.

Suddenly Travis's bike leaped into the air and landed with a bump, swerving dangerously to the left. *"Watch out! Stiiiiiiiiiickssh!"* he cried.

"Stiiiiiiiiicks!" echoed Ben as he swung left and right and left again.

I copied him exactly so that my wheels missed the long branches lying in the middle of the road. I tinkled my bell to thank Travis—he must have known that with Noah in the basket behind me, I would never have been able to stop us from falling over if we had hit them.

From up ahead, Travis tinkled his bell back to say "You're welcome," and we all fell quiet so that we could concentrate harder on the road ahead of us.

We carried on in silence as the hedges around us got smaller again and the trees and fields reappeared. And as the minutes kept ticking by, my legs felt heavier and heavier, my breathing got louder and louder, and the road became harder and harder to ride on. A large drop of sweat made its way slowly down the side of my face and melted into the strap of Sophie's helmet. I wished that the ground would slope downward all the way to London so that we could get there quicker instead of tilting upward like it was doing now. The computer map hadn't said anything about roads being full of bumps and hills and mini-mountains and snake-sticks and how all those things could make us even later!

I stretched my fingers out to ring Mrs. Iwuchukwu's bell and ask if we could stop for a drink of water, then paused. The road had suddenly begun to tremble beneath my wheels and I could hear the roar of a machine behind me. A second later, two huge beams of light swerved around the bend and flashed a warning onto the hedges around me.

"*Caaaaaaaaaaaaaaaaaaaaaaaaaaaaar!*" I screamed, swerving the bike straight into the hedge as the car zoomed past me. I felt a million sharp branches tear at my face and hands as the bike bounced against a cushion of leaves and pushed me and Noah back out toward the road, as if the hedge was annoyed with us for disturbing it. I could feel Noah's basket coming loose and knew exactly what was going to happen next. Launching myself out of the saddle, I reached back to grab Noah and the fluttering white sheet of his costume and pull him toward me. As he landed on top of me with a thud and a whimper, the road smashed itself against my back, kicking the breath from my lungs. We both lay there silently as I tried to breathe normally again. From somewhere up ahead, I heard a screech, a thud, the sound of wheels scraping, and a loud "Aggggggh!" followed by an angry beep.

"Beep you!" I heard Ben shout.

Pushing myself and Noah back upright, I quickly looked around. The car had faded into the dark as if it had never existed, and Travis and Ben were peeling themselves away from the hedge. They hadn't fallen over like me and Noah had.

"Everyone OK?" asked Ben, running up to us.

"A-Aniyah?" asked Travis, sounding worried.

But I didn't answer, because even in the dark I could see that Noah's ghost sheet was torn and his bottom lip was quivering and that he was wiping his eyes. There was a long red scratch mark on his cheek from where one of the sharp branches on the hedge had scraped him through a colander hole.

"Does it hurt, Noah?" I asked, trying to get close to his face so that I could see better.

He nodded. I could tell that he was trying to be brave because he wasn't scream-crying like he usually would be.

I licked one of my tiger paws and used it to wipe the scratch, just like Mum always did whenever Noah fell down in the park. She was always licking things and wiping us with them when we got hurt.

"Ewwwwww!" cried Noah, pushing my hand away and wiping my wipe off, just like he used to do with Mum. For some reason, that made me happy and sad all at the same time.

"Hey, you don't think that was the police or anyone with the services, do you?" asked Ben, looking up at the road ahead. But it was completely dark and empty again.

"Nah, they would have sh-shtopped," said Travis, frowning at me. "Aniyah, are you sure you're OK?"

"Yeah." I shrugged, lying. I could feel a pain shooting up my left ankle and something tingling across my cheeks and my chin, but I didn't want to say anything in case it meant we had to go back.

"But . . . your face," said Ben, pointing at it. "And your . . ." He pointed down at my hands.

Noah stopped rubbing his eyes and looked up at my face too.

"What?" I asked, lifting my hands. I could see there were lots of tiny red scratches all over the top of them—as if an invisible angry cat had attacked me with its claws. I lifted my fingers to my face and carefully touched my cheeks. One side was full of scratches. So was my chin.

"It doesn't hurt," I promised, feeling thankful that it

wasn't daytime yet and none of us could see the scratches. "I can just wash it off later." Ignoring the horrible pain in my ankle, I pulled the bike up toward me and got back on it.

"Come on! Let's keep going!" I said, making my voice sound normal. We had to keep going—we couldn't stop now. "Can you help put Noah back in?" I asked, trying to stop my eyes from watering. "And how far away are we from London?" I wheeled the bike away from the hedge, looking behind me to make sure the road was empty.

"S-still a long way," said Travis as he made sure the basket was safe and placed Noah back inside it. "We're n-nearly at O-Oxford. But it'sh almost n-nine o'clock."

"Race you to London, then!" I shouted, pedaling as fast as my ankle would let me and trying to stop my face from wincing.

Travis and Ben ran over to their bikes and in a few moments were ahead of me again. I could see something glowing blue and gray from the front of Travis's handles and wondered what it was. In the dark, it looked like a phone, but I knew he didn't have one, so it had to be something else. I told my brain to remember to ask him what it was the next time we stopped.

As we carried on cycling, I could feel the pain in my ankle getting sharper, and Sophie's helmet on my head getting stickier, and the cuts on my hands and face feeling sting-ier. Ben and Travis had been singing and talking before, but now they were silent and felt far away, as if we were all cycling in different worlds that only looked the same. I wished there were some road signs to let us know where we were and how far we had to go and how many hills we had left to cycle over, but there was nothing. Just the never-ending lines of prickly bushes that made the dark road look even darker and more unfriendly.

Travis's bike tinkled again as he turned right, into another small lane with no name. As we turned, a loud rumble roared through the sky, and like a black veil being pulled over our heads, the lights of the stars and moon instantly died out. A second later, a large drop of cold water splashed and splattered on the tip of my nose.

"*Danging dingbats!*" cried Ben, lifting his hood. "*It's raining! Travis! It's raining!*"

"*I know!*" Travis shouted back as he cycled even faster. "*F-follow me!*"

Telling my legs they had to work harder than they had ever worked before in their whole lives and shouting at Noah to sit tight, I bowed my head down low and pushed on. From above, as if a giant had opened his front door and was throwing out endless buckets of water, a torrent of rain began to pour down.

As our clothes became wetter and heavier, our bikes became harder to ride. The road, which had been dry and clear, changed into a slippery black stream, and the rain-drops made Ben's and Travis's bike lights fade away. We fought against the sudden freezing wind that had joined in, our faces and our fingers feeling even more numb and cold. My ankle was screaming and my bike was beginning to fall behind and my eyes couldn't see Travis or Ben any-more, but just when I thought I couldn't push the pedals down even one more time, Travis cried out, *"Here!"* and, ringing his bell as loud as he could, turned right.

As soon as we turned, the road became wider and smoother. A large sign saying WELCOME TO THE CITY OF OXFORD was directly ahead. We whizzed past it, and soon there were streetlamps and closed shops throwing out light from their shop signs and a bus in the distance on the op-posite side of the road flashing orange and red lights.

Ringing his bell loudly, Travis jumped off his bike and, running beside it, headed for a large building with steps leading up to lots of pillars. Next to it was a narrow lane lit up by a single lamppost with a blue-and-white sign that said LOGIC LANE.

"Up here!" ordered Travis, pointing to the dry tiles that lay behind the pillars, in front of a large wooden door.

We leaned our tired bikes against a wall, then ran up the

steps and stood huddled and shivering together, watching as the rains crashed down.

"How long should we wait?" asked Ben, rubbing his hands together and blowing into them.

Travis shrugged. "Until it s-stopsh raining."

Ben nodded as Noah clung to my leg and made a noise like a puppy wanting to go home.

"But . . . that might not be for hours," I said, hoping that I was wrong and that the rain would stop immediately.

"Yeah," said Travis quietly as a loud silver flash lit up the sky. He took a step back and sat down against the wooden door. "But we can't r-ride in this. We have to w-wait."

I looked out at the pounding street and the large drops of rain that splashed to their deaths in front of me. I knew we were probably never going to make it to the royal star hunters and their computers on time now. Even if the rain stopped and all the stars came out to guide us, my ankle still felt broken and time was going too fast. Our top-secret mission had failed and I had failed Mum's star. And there was nothing I could do about it.

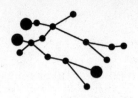

14

The Night of Four Tales

"Man! Isn't this rain ever gonna stop?" asked Ben as he grabbed another handful of sweets from his treat bag. He offered me some, but I shook my head. My throat had closed up again and it wouldn't let me eat anything. Not even sour cola bottles.

None of us had an answer for Ben's question, so we all just sat and stared. Noah's head started to roll slowly down my arm as he gave a soft snore. Pushing his head back up, I took his space helmet off and made my shoulder stiffer so that he wouldn't fall again. I looked down to check his trousers. The bottoms were wet from the rain, but his ghost costume had covered most of him and his trousers were still dry in the middle. That was good, because it meant he hadn't wet himself yet.

"So what do we do now?" asked Ben, on his third handful of sweets. Travis was resting his chin on his knees and looking straight ahead, too tired to reply.

I opened my mouth. But my closed-up throat wouldn't let me say the words *We have to keep going.*

Travis pulled out a small black object from his coat pocket and held it out to us. It was Mrs. Iwuchukwu's sat-nav. So *that's* how Travis had known which roads to take and why he had never had to use our map.

"I can't believe you took that." Ben grinned, shaking his head. "Mrs. I. is going to flip her mattresses when she sees it's gone."

Travis shrugged. "I saw it ch-charging in the kitchen and th-thought it might help. Anyway, I'm only b-borrowing it." He pressed the On button, making a cartoon head of a bald man with large eyebrows and a big grin wave out at us, and the words *Dynamo-Dom—With You Every Step of the Way* flashed above him. After a few seconds, he disappeared, and a wide blue line surrounded by lots of little gray ones appeared on the screen. In the middle was a white arrow that looked like a paper plane pointing to where we were. Next to it were the words *The Examination Schools.*

I looked over my shoulder at the huge door behind us.

I didn't know there were whole schools that made you only do exams! I reminded myself never to go to one of them.

Travis pointed to the numbers at the bottom of the Dynamo-Dom screen. My heart rocketed when I saw that it said *1:38 hours* on one side and *51 miles* on the other, but sank again when Travis said, "That's the c-car time. For our b-bikes it'sh more than d-double."

Ben nodded as I stared at the tiny screen.

"S-sorry, Aniyah," said Travis. "I d-don't think we're gonna get there in time. . . ."

I nodded and bit my tongue angrily. I might have made it to the star hunters on time if I had left yesterday when I knew what I had to do, and had never let anyone join me!

"Mrs. I. is gonna kill us," said Ben, pulling at a strawberry lace with his teeth. "But if she does," he added, "I'm just gonna remind her that she used to run away all the time when she was one of us."

I looked over at Ben, feeling surprised and confused. The surprise made my voice come back, and I heard it ask, "What do you mean? Was she a foster kid too?"

"Yup! And she was really naughty too," said Ben, leaning forward so that he could see me better. "She used to run away all the time 'cause she hated everyone—and then she got given a really nice foster mum and she decided that's what she was going to be when she grew up. That's why she's mega nice to us."

"But—how did she become a foster kid?" I asked, wondering why she had never told me and Noah that she had been like us once.

"Her mum got too sick to look after her, and no one else wanted her," said Ben. "She got given away and became a foster kid. Then her mum died and she tried to get adopted, but she couldn't 'cause by then she was too old, so she kept running away instead."

"She was too old?" I asked, frowning.

"Yeah," said Ben. "Only young foster kids get adopted. If you're a baby, you're sure to get adopted. But once you're older and become a teenager, no one wants you because you've got hormones and spots and stuff coming out, and you get too tall. That's why me and Travis are trying to make Mrs. I. adopt us. We're getting too old and tall too, so it's kind of like our last chance."

I looked at Travis. He opened his eyes and gave me a nod, as if being tall was something he wished he could change.

"Mrs. I. wanted her own kids as well as foster kids," added Ben, stuffing another strawberry lace in his mouth. "Af'er she go- mawwied -o Mi-her Iwu-chuk-wu." Gulping hard again, he added, "But Mr. Iwuchukwu and her couldn't have any, see, and then Mr. I. got cancer and died, so she became a foster mum."

"Oh," I whispered, not knowing what else to say. Now I understood why Mrs. Iwuchukwu smiled so much and never told Noah off for wetting the bed or for screaming and crying. I also felt even more worried than I was before—because what if Mrs. Iwuchukwu didn't believe that running away to London was my idea and decided to make Travis and Ben stay foster kids forever? What if I had made them lose their last chance of being adopted by letting them come with me to find Mum's star? A very large and real lump began to grow in the back of my throat.

"But you and N-Noah don't need to worry," said Travis. "Noah's little and p-people like taking b-brothersh and sistersh together."

"Why hasn't Mrs. Iwuchukwu adopted you yet?" I asked. "You're both much nicer than Sophie is! She should have adopted you and not her."

Travis shook his head and Ben said, "Nah. Sophie's been with Mrs. I. since she was six! Me and Travis only came last year. Travis came first, and then I came about two weeks after him. It's not enough time yet for her to want to adopt us for good."

"Yeah," agreed Travis, looking at his knees again.

We all stayed quiet for a moment, and then I asked the question I had been wanting to ask ever since my first night at Mrs. Iwuchukwu's house. "But so how come you're both foster kids? Did your mums and dads disappear too?" I asked.

Travis and Ben both silently looked at each other, as if each of them was asking the other one if they should tell me. They both must have said yes, because Ben looked back at me and said, "I turned into one because Mum and Dad couldn't take care of me and my sister anymore."

"Oh!" I said, nodding. I made my face stay the same, even though my mouth wanted to fall open and my eyes wanted to stare at him even harder. Ben had a sister! And a mum and dad too.

Ben looked down and talked into his hood as if it had asked him the question and not me. "Dad used to be a deliveryman," he continued. "With his own van and everything. And whenever he was happy, he would take us to see all the football matches. He gave me this," he said, touching his hoodie. "Because we supported Newcastle United. That's where he was from."

I nodded. I had a favorite sweater too. Mum and Dad had bought it for me from Disneyland. It had been a *Lion King* one with photographs of lions—real ones, not cartoon ones—with golden glitter in their eyes. If I still had it, I would wear it all the time as well.

"But then, when he lost his job and his business got shut down, Dad got really sad," continued Ben. He gave a sniff, as if his nose was running. "And that was when he started going out to the pub a lot. When he came back, he would yell at all of us and hurt Mum. . . . Then, one day, Mum told him to go away and never come back, and he hurt us all so much that me and my sister got taken away and put in lots of different foster homes with lots of different foster parents. We didn't like most of them, so we kept running away. But when we came to Mrs. I.'s, I liked it, so I stayed. . . ."

"And your sister?" I asked, hoping she didn't live too far from Mrs. Iwuchukwu's house.

"She didn't like living in foster homes," said Ben, giving an even louder sniff. "So she ran away again. But she's eighteen now, so she can live on her own. She moved to Wales and she . . . she doesn't like seeing me because it gives her bad memories. That's it, really." Ben still hadn't looked up from his sweater.

"Oh," I said again, wondering where Ben's real mum was and if she was OK now. But I knew that he didn't want me to ask him any more questions, so I stayed quiet.

Travis's eyes looked over Noah's head at me as I waited

for him to say something. He opened his mouth and then, looking over at Ben, said, "Ben, you t-tell it."

Ben gave a small nod and said, "Travis's mum died when he was seven—she was ill, and he was with her all alone when it happened. His dad had left when he was still a baby, so the care people made him live with his aunt for a bit. But she wasn't nice to him, so one day he got taken away from her and put into foster homes, and that's where he's been ever since." Ben finished with a shrug, as if what he was saying was all pretty normal.

I looked up at Travis, but I couldn't see his eyes anymore. His hair had dropped down over his face, and he was looking at his knees and flicking something invisible away from the top of them with his fingers. Now I knew why Travis had asked what it had sounded like when his mum's heart had left her body to go and turn into a star.

"He doesn't like talking about it," said Ben. "Because the doctors say that's how he got his stutter. His aunt gave it to him."

I frowned, wondering how someone could give someone else a stutter. Noah used to stutter sometimes, but only if he was too scared to tell Mum and Dad that he'd been naughty and broken something. And then he'd go right back to normal afterward.

"His *aunt* gave him a stutter?" I asked.

Ben nodded. "Yeah . . . you know . . . by making him too frightened to get his words out. Sometimes when Sophie's being extra mean, she makes him stutter more."

Travis gave a loud sniff, just like Ben had done.

"Why is Sophie so mean to everyone?" I asked, thinking of my spaghetti bowl and her I-hate-you stares and my locket. When I thought of her making Travis stutter more, it made me hate her even more than I already did. I had never met anyone who was as mean as her.

"B-because she's scared we'll be adopted too," said Travis quietly.

Ben nodded. "She was like us once—a foster kid. But then Mrs. I. loved her and adopted her, and Sophie doesn't want her to love or adopt anyone else. I guess she's scared that Mrs. I. will love them more than her or will care about her less. She tries to make everyone leave by being horrible to them, even though she knows what it feels like not to have a real family. Her dad died when she was small and her mum didn't want her, so she gave Sophie away. She went to some other foster homes and had foster mums and dads, but then Mrs. I. took her when she was six and she never left. She got *really* lucky."

"Yeah," said Travis as he finally flicked away his hair so we could see his face again. His eyes looked extra shiny.

I stayed sitting quietly, wondering about everything I

had heard. I had never heard of mums giving their children away before, or people being so horrible that they could give you a stutter, or dads who hurt mums so much they made everyone split up. All of it seemed horrible and unfair.

Laying my head on top of Noah's, I wondered where Dad was and why he hadn't come to find us yet. He always said he was a family man, so I knew he wouldn't like us not being a family anymore. At the hotel-that-wasn't-really-a-hotel, Mum had said we needed to stay hiding from Dad for a long time. But now that she had left, I was sure that wasn't true, and as soon as he found us, I would ask him to help Ben and Travis get adopted quickly so they wouldn't need to worry anymore.

My thoughts were cut short as a large red coach stopped in front of us, splashing the steps with rainwater and making all of us tuck our legs in tightly to our chests. The coach was brightly lit and had lots of people inside, some sleeping with their heads squashed against the windows. The double doors hissed open and someone covering their head with a coat got out and ran down Logic Lane.

As the coach closed its doors and began to drive away, Travis sat up straight. "Look!" he ordered, pointing to the back of the coach excitedly.

I leaned forward and quickly read the giant letters

written diagonally across the back of the coach before they faded away. They said:

```
OXFORD TUBE
FROM EVERY 10 MINUTES
24 HOURS A DAY
OXFORD–LONDON
FROM £8 RETURN
```

"That's it!" cried out Ben, thumping Travis on the arm. "Let's get on the coach to London!"

I sat up, feeling so excited that I accidentally forgot about Noah's head and felt it rolling off my shoulder. Catching it, I pushed it back on again.

"Could we?" I asked. If we caught the coach right away, we might still make it to London before midnight! "Will we have enough money for tickets?"

Travis nodded. "Yeah, we should! Me and B-Ben have got all our m-money with us. B-but we'll need to wait until the m-morning—when there's more p-people and the d-drivers won't call the police on ush!"

"Yeah," agreed Ben, shaking his bag and making the coins he had inside it jingle. "And the coach will be much safer than cycling—especially if Mrs. I.'s called the police and we're wanted criminals now! Plus we won't get knocked down by any more stupid cars," he added.

"But—the competition ends tonight. It'll be too late in the morning," I reminded them. "The star hunters won't be there after it gets light—they only work when the stars are out at night, remember? And if they're not there, we won't have anyone to tell about Mum's star. It's better if we go now!"

Travis shook his head. "It's t-too late for us to g-get on one now. There won't be anyone our a-age out this late— even on Halloween! But if we go in the m-morning," he said, getting excited, "we can still m-make it in time for the gala p-party! Remember? The computers will pick the name at midnight, but nobody will know what it ish until the p-party tomorrow!"

I looked down at Noah and thought hard. Ben and Travis were right. The website *had* said the name for Mum's star wouldn't be announced until the gala . . . which meant we would have the whole day to get to the star hunters and make sure they used Mum's real name for her star and not a pretend one chosen by the computers. I knew Mum wouldn't want to be called by the wrong name, but I also knew she wouldn't mind waiting just a little bit longer for me to fix everything. We still had a chance. Just as long as Mrs. Iwuchukwu and the police didn't catch us!

"OK," I said, trying to stop myself from running after the coach—even in the rain. "Let's go as soon as it's morning!"

"Let's g-get some sleep firsht," said Travis as he pulled the hood of his skeleton costume over his head.

Ben nodded, and whispered, "Mrs. I. is sooo gonna kill us. . . ." Then he wrapped his cloak around himself and placed his Darth Vader mask over his face to protect it from the rain.

Next to me, Noah gave another sigh and rolled his head over to Travis's arm.

I wanted to sleep too because my eyes were feeling like my ankle—all swollen and sore and strange. But every time I closed my eyes, I kept thinking about the tales of Mrs. Iwuchukwu and Ben and Travis and Sophie, and wondering how many foster kids and foster parents and foster houses there were in the world, and why I had never heard about any of them before I had to become one and live in one. So I kept my eyes open and looked out at the rain splashing on the steps in front of me until, as if someone was sticking fluffy cotton into my ears, the sound of the raindrops began to fade away. My eyelids soon became too heavy to keep open, and without knowing when, I gave in and felt myself being sucked into a big black hole of sleep.

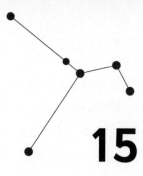

15

Unusual and Suspicious Articles

"Oi! What you lot doing here?"

My eyes tore open and stared at the strange man look-ing down at me. Dressed in bright yellow trousers and a jacket that was the same color as Dad's highlighting pens, the man was staring at me through a bushy white beard and even bushier eyebrows and holding a large wooden brush like a walking stick.

I blinked and tried to wake my brain up, because I didn't know where I was or if I was still sleeping. Sitting up, I saw Noah's space helmet roll off my knees and clatter onto the tiled floor. Suddenly I remembered! We were in Oxford—and we had to catch the coach and get to Lon-don before the gala tonight!

"I said! What you lot doing here? Halloween's *over!* And what? What's this little one doing here? *Eh?"*

Jumping to his feet, Travis quickly grabbed his bag and kicked Ben with his foot to wake him up.

"S-sorry, sir," he said as I shook Noah awake. "We-we got lost on the way h-home from t-trick-or-t-treating! We're v-vishiting . . ."

"Our—er, grandparents," said Ben from beneath his Darth Vader mask.

Pulling Noah to his feet, I nodded too. But now that Noah was awake, he was beginning to cry. He was too tired to know what was going on and he wanted Mum.

"Don't worry, Noah, we're going to Nana's right now!" I said, grabbing his hand and my rucksack and standing up. My ankle felt even more swollen and sore than it had last night. Trying to blink away the pain, I limped down the stairs as quickly as I could.

The man watched us with a frown as we grabbed our bikes and hurried away down the road. I didn't know if we were even going the right way, but it didn't matter. We just had to go somewhere the man couldn't see us. I looked over my shoulder and saw him watching us, shaking and scratching his head. I gave him a wave and tried to smile. He stared at me, his face folding into lots of creases, before finally going back to brushing the tiles we had been sleeping on.

Noah began to cry and cling on to my leg, making it harder for me to walk.

"Noah, shhhhhh! Remember, we're going to help name Mum's star—remember! We're on an adventure!"

"Here," said Travis as he picked Noah up and put him on the high seat of his bike. "Hold on to the handlesh, Noah!" he ordered.

Noah instantly stopped crying and clung to the handles, looking excited.

"Want some, Noah?" asked Ben, pulling a packet of crisps from his hoodie. Noah wiped away his tears and happily grabbed a handful. Cramming them into his mouth, he started to hum, which meant he was happy.

"Where'd you g-get them?" asked Travis, frowning.

"I dunno." Ben shrugged. "Found them in my gym bag. I've eaten everything in my treat bag. Anyone want to share their—"

"Wait! Aniyah! What'sh wrong with your f-foot?" asked Travis, making us all stop.

"Nothing!" I lied, trying to put my right foot down all the way on the ground. But it hurt too much, and I instantly stood back up on my toes.

"Whoa!" said Ben, bending down to take a look. "Aniyah! It looks like you've grown a plum!"

I looked down and twisted my leg around so that I could see my ankle properly. Ben was right. It had swollen up into a horrible watery ball after I had fallen asleep, and turned a strange kind of purple blue. It really did look like a plum.

"You're hurt," said Travis. "We need to g-go to the hos-hospital!"

"*No!*" I shouted—even though I hadn't meant to shout at all. "Please! I'm fine! I just need to . . ." But I didn't know what I needed to do to make the pain go away. So I said, "I just need to walk on it like this!" I rolled my bike past him, walking on the tiptoe of my hurt foot, and normally with the other.

"See? Doesn't hurt that much! It just looks bad, that's all!"

"You sure?" asked Ben, not looking sure at all.

"Promise," I said, hoping my smile looked real. "Come on—please! Let's go!"

Nodding, Ben and Travis followed me down the road. After a minute of half tiptoeing and half walking past closed shops and cafés, I stopped. We had come to the corner of a road that split into four ways. In front of us was a small church with a clock that told us it was nearly a quarter to eight. Which meant we had just over eleven hours to get to London, find the star hunters, and stop the competition.

"Travis, are we going the right way?"

"Oh!" said Travis, reaching for the satnav in his pocket, then stopping and pointing up instead. "Yup! We're going the right way!" Above our heads was a long black pole with lots of white arrow signs sticking out in different directions. Pointing straight ahead was one that said COACH STATION 500 YARDS.

Rolling our bikes down the road past more shops and restaurants, we began to hear the humming and growling of engines and people and cars. The empty streets were starting to fill up, and the closer we got to the coach station, the more and more people we began to see.

"Why is everyone staring?" whispered Ben as we entered a large square where lots of people were setting up market stalls.

I looked around. Ben was right—wherever we walked, grown-ups were looking at us with frowns and beady shining eyes.

I shrugged, but then I saw a woman walking with a box of books stop in her tracks to stare at Ben and Travis.

Of course!

"It's our costumes!" I whispered, realizing how weird

it must be for everyone to see a tiger, a skeleton, Darth Vader, and a small ghost with a colander on its head walking the streets when it wasn't Halloween anymore.

"Oh yeah!" said Ben, pulling off his Darth Vader mask and stuffing it into his rucksack.

Me and Travis looked at each other with a worried frown on our faces, because we didn't have anything else we could change into.

"No!" shouted Noah, pushing my hand away from him as I tried to take the colander from his head and pull his ghost costume off.

"Look, there's toilets over there," said Ben, pointing to a metal sign. "I need to go! Let's all go and get cleaned up." I nodded, and Ben and Travis leaned their bikes against a shop wall and hurried inside.

"I want to go too!" moaned Noah, pushing my hand away from his arm.

"Noah, no! You can't! That's the big boys' toilet!"

"I don't care! I want to *go*!" And breaking free from me, Noah dashed into the men's toilet too. It was the first time he had left me to go and do something on his own since Mum had left. I felt worried, but I was also glad that he had two bigger brothers to help him.

After a few minutes of watching the toilet doors and trying to pretend that I wasn't, Travis and Ben came out with Noah skipping up and down behind them. He still had his space helmet on, but he wasn't in his ghost sheet anymore and had chocolate stains all over his face.

"Thanks," I said as Travis gave me Noah's ghost sheet to pack into my rucksack. "I—I need to go too," I said. Travis nodded and held my bike while I went in and washed my face and my hands. Looking into the mirror scared me at first, because I had forgotten about the scratches on my face. They had all dried overnight and made me look like a tiger that had been in a catfight. I washed them and wiped my ankle with cold water, because it felt like it was burning. The plum had turned even darker now, but I didn't want Travis and Ben to stop me because of it, so I pulled down my tiger legs to hide it.

Feeling more awake, I joined Travis and Ben and we rolled our bikes to the coach area.

"Wow," I said, looking at the row of shiny red and orange and green and purple buses standing diagonally in a long neat line, just like airplanes at the airport.

"We need that r-red one," said Travis, pointing to where a large double-decker Oxford Tube coach stood. It had the words *London Victoria Station* flashing orange on its front window, which made my heart feel like it was flashing too.

"How we going to get on?" asked Ben, looking around

nervously. "Do you think we've really got enough money for all our tickets?"

Travis nodded. "I've about got twenty-three pounds. And if the tickets are eight pounds each, we'd need . . ." Travis quickly spread his fingers like a fan again. But before he could say anything, I shouted out, "Thirty-two pounds!" I wasn't a human computer yet—I had counted how much we needed last night as soon as we saw the coach sign. But Travis looked impressed.

"Yeah, thirty-two pounds. How much do you have?" he asked, looking at Ben.

"Seven pounds twenty-three," said Ben.

"What?" asked Travis, looking shocked. "Mrs. I. gave you a tenner on Wednesday! I thought you still had it!"

"I got some stickers and had a chip roll." Ben frowned. "I didn't know we'd need it for this, did I? And Mrs. I.'s got my savings card!"

Travis shook his head as an old man and an old woman walked by holding hands. They looked like two happy penguins and gave us a smile as they passed. The smile was big at first, but when they saw my face and my slightly muddy tail, their smiles turned into frowns.

"Come on," said Travis, his eyes following the old couple who were glancing back at us now and whispering to each other. "Let'sh hurry!"

Making our way to the back of the long line of coaches, we found a big pillar right behind the coach we needed to get on. Leaning our bikes and helmets against the pillar, we watched everything that was happening in front of us. Noah and me had never been to a coach station before—we had been on a coach for school trips, but Mum and Dad had always driven us everywhere else. It felt exciting and was just like being at an airport—except it didn't have any gates or conveyor belts and everything was outside. The coach drivers looked a bit like pilots, though, because they all had white shirts and jackets that matched the colors of their coaches—but they also shouted a lot and helped people with their suitcases, which airplane pilots never do.

"If we don't have enough money for tickets, how are we going to get on?" I asked, hoping Ben would know the answer since he had run away lots of times before. But he just shrugged.

"I've never run away on a coach," he said. "I got on a train once, but . . ."

Travis grinned. "But he got too s-scared and got off after t-two stopsh!"

"Yeah, well, it was scary!" said Ben, looking at me as if he wanted me to believe him. "I was only eight! *And* I was on my own!"

I nodded, because I knew I would have been scared

too. Trying to run away forever was much scarier than trying to run away just for a night.

I watched the coach drivers some more, trying to think about what to do. And then slowly my brain began to notice a pattern. The driver in front of us was doing it, and the driver of the green coach on the left was doing it too, and so was the driver of the purple coach way on the right. . . .

They were all following the same pattern! Suddenly, I had the answer to my own question about how we could get on a coach without any money!

I poked Travis and Ben on the arm to see if they had seen the pattern too, but they just looked at me with an "Oh no!" and a frown.

"Look!" I said, pulling on Travis's coat sleeve. "Look at what the driver's doing!"

"Which one?" asked Travis and Ben together as Noah leaned forward and pushed back his space helmet so that he could see too.

"That one," I said, pointing straight at the Oxford Tube coach we needed to get on. "See? As soon as he's got everyone's tickets, he makes everyone with the big cases go and stand over there and lets everyone without any suitcases go on!"

"Yeah, so?" asked Ben.

"Look." We waited until the driver had finished taking

everyone's tickets, and watched as he walked to the side of the coach where the people with extra-big suitcases were waiting. One by one, he looked at their tickets again, and put the suitcases into a special place.

"See?" I asked, feeling so excited that my legs were shaking. I was glad Noah's arms were wrapped around one of them.

"No!" said Ben.

I rolled my eyes. "Look!" I said, pointing back to the coach. "Look at the doors! They're *open*!" I couldn't wait any longer for them to guess the answer. "He's left them *open* while he goes and checks the suitcase people's tickets. Which means . . ."

"We can—we can get in from the f-front!" finished Travis.

I nodded as Noah pulled on my sleeve, rubbing his eyes. He was getting tired again.

"Not long now, Noah, I promise," I said, giving him a squeeze. Noah nodded and then jumped as the driver of the coach in front of us slammed the suitcase door shut with a bang, climbed back into the front seat, and let the suitcase people on. Then, with a shudder and a roar, the coach puffed a large cloud of black smoke into our faces and moved away.

"That's a *big* fart!" said Noah, looking impressed.

"Yup, and we're going to hear even bigger ones if you promise not to cry and to listen to everything I say, OK?" I said, making Noah nod so fast that his head looked like one of Ben's bobbleheads.

"Look! The next one is already here!" said Ben as another bright red Oxford Tube coach beeped and flashed and drove backward into the space to replace the one that had just left.

"Wait . . . ," said Travis, frowning at something over his shoulder. "What are we g-going to do with our b-bikesh?"

"Huh?" asked Ben, looking panicked. Then, seeing the answer in Travis's eyes, he gave a groan. "Aw, man! We can't leave them here! They'll get stolen—or taken away by the police!"

We looked down at our bikes as if they were pets we didn't want to leave behind.

"We have to," said Travis quietly.

After a few seconds, Ben shook his head and gave his bike saddle a sad pat. "This sucks, Newky." Looking up at me and Travis, he added, "If we ever get home, I'm going to *ask* to go to jail. 'Cause Mrs. I.'s definitely gonna kill us now."

Travis gave his bike a quick pat too, then helped Ben lean his bike against it and then Mrs. Iwuchukwu's. It felt horrible, but no matter how hard I tried to think of another way, I knew we couldn't get on the coach with the bikes, and we couldn't use them to cycle to London because of my ankle. I promised myself that when we got back, I would save up for the rest of my life to buy both Travis and Ben the best bikes ever built in the whole entire universe. And a bike with an even bigger basket for Mrs. Iwuchukwu.

"Noah, you have to stay with me and be super fast so we can get to Mum, OK?" I whispered as we waited by the pillar, ready to run onto the coach when the driver's back was turned. I held Noah's hand tight as a new group of people lined up to get on our coach.

"OK!" said Noah, puffing out his chest and making his ready face—which meant squeezing it so much that it looked like a squashed lemon. Pulling his space helmet on even tighter, he waited.

We watched as what seemed like a million people began to squeeze themselves up to the front doors of the coach, with some people coming back out like rejected fish to stand beside a pool of suitcases.

"Ready?" whispered Travis as he stood up straighter, seeming to grow taller too.

Ben gulped and gave a nod.

Finally, the driver climbed down from the coach and went to the side door. Opening it with the press of a button and a loud hiss, she started taking the suitcases from the group of people who had instantly surrounded her.

I waited for Travis or Ben to say "Go!" but they didn't move. And then, before I even had time to ask them why, the driver was already shutting the doors and heading back to her seat.

"Next one!" promised Ben as we all watched the coach pull away and waited for another one to come and take its place. But we didn't move for that one either—or the one after that—because each time the driver seemed bigger and scarier, and our legs felt as if they were never going to be fast enough.

"This time!" promised Ben again as the fourth coach came to a stop in front of us. We all watched as once more the driver took everyone's tickets and then began to load the suitcases.

"Now!" I whispered, because I could tell that Travis and Ben were still waiting and I knew that they were going to wait too long! Breaking away from the pillar, I half ran and half hopped as fast as I could down the empty side of the coach and over to the large front window. Stopping by the big yellow number plate, I made Noah stop too, and peeked around the edge. The driver was still busy with the suitcases and couldn't see us at all!

"Quick!" I whispered as I pressed my back up against

the coach's face and, turning the corner, pulled Noah up the steps. We were inside!

Instantly, two pairs of eyes from the front seats of the coach looked at me and Noah, but then looked away again. Rushing past them, I made my way to the stairs and, grabbing my tiger tail, hopped up each one until we got to the top floor. I wanted to look behind me to make sure that Ben and Travis were there, but my body was too scared to let me slow down.

I saw three rows of seats in the back that looked empty and hurried toward them. Pulling Noah into a seat by the window, I put his seat belt on for him and told him we were playing hide-and-seek again, just like we had with Mum. "So you have to keep your head down, OK?" I said. "Like this!" And sitting down, I showed him how to put his head low, as if he was sleeping.

I watched for Ben and Travis so that I could wave at them and show them where we were. But first a grown-up man came up, and then a woman, and then another three men, and then a girl and her grandmother, and then . . . no one.

Suddenly I heard a bang—the side door of the coach was being closed!

I watched the stairs again and crossed my fingers and toes. But there was still no Ben or Travis!

Then, like a snoring monster being woken up, the coach shuddered beneath our seats and came to life. Feeling the coach move backward, I felt my stomach twist itself into a hurricane. Were Ben and Travis about to be run over? Had they stayed hidden behind the pillar? What if they had been caught and arrested by the station police just as they were about to get on?

A clicking sound echoed all around us as a woman's voice came on the speakers: "Ladies and gentlemen, welcome to the nine-twenty Oxford Tube service calling at all stops to London Victoria Station. Please ensure luggage is stowed safely and securely in the allocated storage facilities and inform the driver of any unusual or suspicious articles."

Noah looked up at me, his space helmet shaking as much as the coach. I knew he was getting frightened and wanted to know where Ben and Travis were too, but I put my finger to my lips and warned him to stay quiet because we were both unusual and suspicious articles now.

With a great big swerve, the coach lunged forward, making me grip the seat and Noah's hands tightly. We were finally on our way to London . . . but without Travis or Ben. And even though I still had Noah with me, I had never felt more frightened or alone.

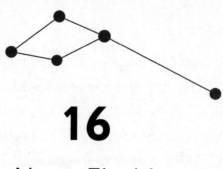

16

News Flash!

As soon as the coach left the station, I looked around for an idea of what to do. I wanted to run to the back window to see if I could see Travis and Ben anywhere, but there were two men sitting there now and I couldn't be even more suspicious and unusual than I already was—not when I was dressed as a girl-tiger and sitting next to a boy with a colander on his head. The grandmother and the little girl were sitting on the seats in front of me and Noah, and I was sure they had looked at us strangely before they had sat down. Maybe they already knew we didn't have any tickets and were illegal criminals.

As the coach moved faster and faster and faster and the roads outside our window got bigger and wider, I tried to think about what to do. But the harder I thought, the blanker my brain became—as if someone had cut the electricity and the plug, and it couldn't work anymore.

"Niyah, I'm hungry," moaned Noah as he pulled my arm. "Where's Ben? Can he give us more crisps?"

"Ben's going to meet us in London," I lied, not knowing what else to say.

"But I'm hungry *now*!" whined Noah, his face starting to get red.

"Shhhhhh!"

"No!" cried Noah, his lips shaking. "Where's—hic!—Ben? I—hic!—want Ben!"

"Here!" said a voice from the seat in front of me. Suddenly an arm poked through the gap between the two seats and held out a shiny blue packet at us. "You can have these if you want!"

Noah instantly fell quiet and, still hiccuping, stared at the packet of chocolate-covered pretzels that had appeared in front of him. Then, nodding, he snatched them and waited for me to let him eat them.

"Thank you," I said, leaning into the gap. I could spot a bright green-gray eye looking back at me.

"It's OK," said the eye, before it disappeared, a ball of shiny yellow hair bouncing back into place in the seat in front of me.

"Good girl," came a whisper from the seat next to it. It sounded exactly like the good-girl whispers Mum used to give me when I had done something to make her happy, and it made me want to jump up from my seat and take a look at the person who had said it. But I didn't, because I knew it wasn't Mum.

Instead, I let Noah have the pretzels and tried to think some more. My stomach made a growling noise because I had smelled the chocolate, but I knew I wouldn't be able to eat again until I found out what had happened to Ben and Travis. I should have looked behind to see if they had been following me! And I shouldn't have gotten on the coach at all without them! It was my fault we were split up—and I didn't know how to fix it, or what me and Noah were going to do when we got to London. I didn't have the map or the satnav, or any food or money. But those things didn't seem to matter half as much as not having Ben and Travis with me. They had helped me in ways that nobody else had ever helped me before—even though they knew it might get them into trouble. It didn't feel right to get to the royal star hunters without them. I closed my eyes and made a wish to Mum's star to please, please, and extra please help me find them again.

"The next stop is Thornhill Park and Ride. All

passengers for Thornhill Park and Ride, please alight here," said a woman's voice loudly as the coach swerved left into the middle of a large car park.

I wondered if we should get out and wait for Ben and Travis in the car park—because maybe they had caught the next coach and would want us to wait for them there. But then, what if they hadn't? How long would we wait? And what if me and Noah couldn't get back on another coach? I didn't think the same trick would work in a place that wasn't a coach station.

I was still wondering what to do when the coach began to move again, making Noah press his nose up against the glass and cry, "Yay!"

As the coach bounced along a large motorway, Noah became quiet and finally fell asleep. I felt glad, because it meant I could think without worrying about him. After taking off his space helmet, I pulled out the souvenir guide from my rucksack and looked at the map at the back. If only I could have met them somewhere . . .

But that was it! They knew I had to get to the big gala party before seven o'clock to make sure the star hunters announced the right name for Mum's star! So I knew they would try to get there too. They might even get there quicker because they had Dynamo-Dom to show them the way and I didn't!

Feeling much better, I put the guide away and watched the roads and cars below flash by. But after a short while, the coach began to slow down until eventually it came to a complete stop.

"Great," muttered a voice behind me. "Another traffic jam! Wonder how long this one will last."

The coach didn't move for what felt like a long time.

I closed my eyes tight and told the traffic to please disappear for good so that we could get to London quickly. I still didn't know how to get to the Royal Observatory from there . . . or where the star hunters would be exactly . . . and there was so much to tell them . . . and . . . and . . .

"Niyah . . . Niyah! Wake up! Wake up!"

I opened my eyes and rubbed them quickly. Noah was pulling my arm, and everyone on the coach was getting up and gathering like a swarm of bees at the top of the stairs. Outside the window was a huge blue-and-white sign that said VICTORIA COACH STATION.

"Oh! Thank you, Noah!" I said, quickly undoing his seat belt and mine.

"You fell asleep!" said Noah, shaking his head as if he had caught me doing something naughty.

I nodded, wondering how long I had been asleep and what time it was. Stuffing the space helmet into my rucksack, I grabbed Noah's hand and went to wait behind everyone trying to get down the stairs. The pain in my ankle felt even worse now. But that didn't matter anymore. We were in London and the star hunters weren't too far away now, and Ben and Travis would find us—I knew they would!

"Come on, Noah, quick!" I said, grabbing his hand as we reached the last step. The driver wasn't in her seat and there was no one on the bottom floor anywhere. It was all empty. "We have to go now!"

"Psssssssst! Aniyah!"

I looked around for the voice that was calling my name. It seemed to be coming from the floor of the back of the coach. But all the seats there were empty. Had I imagined it?

All of a sudden, two heads rose up out of a sea of seats. One of them grinned at me—but the other one was covered with a hood, making it look like a strange black triangle.

"Phew! We thought you'd left!" said Ben, pulling his hood down and giving me a grin.

"Yeah!" said Travis, climbing over Ben to get out first.

Feeling so happy that I didn't know what else to do, I ran down the aisle and, ignoring the pain in my ankle, jumped on Travis and Ben so that I could give them the biggest hug I had ever given two people at the same time ever!

"Ouch!" cried Ben.

"Er . . . er . . . ," stuttered Travis.

"Yippeeeeeeeeee!" cried Noah. *"Crisps!"*

"How did you— I thought— Where . . . ?" I wanted to get all my questions out, but there were too many of them.

"We'll t-tell you later!" said Travis as I stood up straight again and let him go. He was blushing so much that he was almost as red as the coach seats. "L-let's go b-before the d-driver comesh back!"

"Yeah," said Ben, his grin so wide that I could see all his teeth. "I can't feel my legs! That traffic jam was the worst."

"OK." I nodded as I turned and hurried down the corridor. Hearing Ben's and Travis's and Noah's footsteps following me from behind, I squeezed my eyes shut for a single moment and sent Mum the biggest thank-you my heart could give her. I knew her star must have heard me making my wishes in the seat upstairs and had made them come true, and that it was her who was making me feel more bubbly and excited than I had ever felt—as if all my insides had been filled with the biggest bottle of fizzy drink in the world!

I jumped off the coach first, trying to ignore the horrible pain in my ankle, then turned to help Noah get down too.

"Hey!" cried out a voice from behind me. "Where'd you lot come from?"

I looked over my shoulder and saw the coach driver staring at me with her mouth open, her hands raised in midair, about to slam the suitcase door shut.

"Quick!" cried Travis as he jumped off the coach and pushed me forward.

"Hey!" cried the coach driver as she came rushing toward us.

"Holy hoovers! Ruuuuuun!" cried Ben, and he jumped in front of us and ran toward the coach station.

"Stop!" cried out the coach driver. *"Stop them!"* Instantly, everyone around us turned to look as we fled as fast as we could from the driver. I couldn't run properly and was slowing down—the pain in my ankle was too much— but I could hear the coach driver's footsteps getting closer and closer!

"Aniyah! Jump up!" cried Travis, and lifted me onto his back to give me a piggyback ride.

"Good idea!" said Ben, doing the same to Noah, and

running even faster than they had before, they crashed through the glass doors of the station and into a crowd of a million people.

The thump, thump, thump of the coach driver's shoes faded, but as I looked over my shoulder, I saw her stop and take out a walkie-talkie and speak into it.

"Faster!" I shouted to Travis. "She's calling the police!"

"This way!" shouted Ben as grown-ups everywhere tutted and muttered, "Oi!"

After running across the whole station and past hundreds of people, we reached a pair of escalators with a sign that read PLATFORMS 17–21 & SHOPPING PLAZA. As we rose higher and higher and were slowly able to see more of the whole station, we looked around for the coach driver and any police. But we couldn't see them anywhere.

"Phew!" said Ben, using his hood to wipe away some of the sweat from his face. "That was close!"

"Yeah!" I said. "Thanks for carrying me, Travis!"

But Travis wasn't looking at me or Ben or Noah. He had turned away from the station floor behind us and was staring at something at the top of the escalators with his mouth and his braces wide open.

Raising a finger, he pointed up and said, "Oh no . . ."

Ben and me turned just as the escalator came to an end, and quickly jumped off.

"Jumping jellytots," whispered Ben as Noah slid down his back onto the floor.

Above us, hanging from the ceiling of a long corridor filled with shops and burger restaurants and sweet stalls, was one of the biggest television screens I had ever seen. And on the screen were giant pictures of four children who looked exactly like me, Noah, Travis, and Ben—but without the messy hair, chocolate stains, or scratch marks. Above our faces, in extra-giant, extra-shiny red letters were the words:

NEWS FLASH: APPEAL FOR MISSING CHILDREN
Runaway children thought to be in pursuit of murder suspect

Noah jumped up and down and, pointing at his face on the screen, shouted, "Niyah! We're famous!"

But I didn't reply. I wanted to know what the news flash meant. "Why would we run away to find a murder suspect?" I asked, frowning.

Travis and Ben looked at each other for a moment. It was only for a second, but I could tell right away they were saying something to each other with their eyes. I didn't know what it was, but I did know that it made them both turn red. After the second was over, Ben turned to me and, laughing for no reason, said, "Who knows! Reporters are crazy! Come on! We'd better move!"

Taking a last look at the screen, I followed Travis and Ben and Noah as they hurried past the endless rows of shops, Travis and Ben still glancing at each other as they went. I couldn't help wondering who the murder suspect was and why the reporters thought we might try to go in pursuit of them. And, most of all, why Ben and Travis had suddenly started to act so unusually and suspiciously.

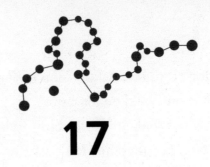

17

Over and Under London's Ground

"Niyah! I'm hungry again," said Noah as he walked alongside us trying to see through the holes in his make-believe helmet. Ben had put his Darth Vader mask back on, while me and Travis had pulled our hoods down as far as they would go over our faces. People still stared at us as we walked past them, but most of them just smiled—I could tell they thought we were still trick-or-treating. At the end of the corridor of shops, a pair of glass doors waited for us, showing a busy road filled with people and cars and trucks and sunlight on the other side. Even though it felt as if my ankle might fall off soon, I couldn't wait to get outside. I was starting to feel dizzy and sick, and I knew some fresh air would make me feel better. Mum said fresh air worked wonders, and always opened the windows when me or Noah were sick so that we could breathe the wonders in.

"Niyaaaah," whined Noah as we came to a stop just next to the doors.

"Shhh, Noah," I said, watching Travis as he quickly got his Dynamo-Dom out and tried to switch it on. But no matter how hard he pressed the button, the screen stayed blank. He tapped it against his leg and he tried again.

"Oh no! The b-batteriesh have gone!" he said, looking as if the satnav had betrayed him.

"Don't worry," I said, taking the Royal Observatory souvenir guide from my bag. I opened it to the map at the back and held it out to Travis and Ben and Noah. "We just need someone to tell us how to get to here. Or here." I pointed to the large pirate ship and then the star hunters' headquarters.

"Will there be food on here?" asked Noah, pointing to the ship too as someone else's stomach growled.

Ben turned bright red and whispered, "Sorry!"

"Wait here!" said Travis, running back toward the shops. After a few minutes, just as me and Ben were starting to get worried, Travis returned, carrying a large white bag filled with four hot croissants.

"Ah, man! You're the best!" cried Ben as he lunged for a croissant and stuffed half of it into his mouth. "It i- d-ish-ush!"

Noah gave a happy squeal. Now that we were getting

closer to the royal star hunters, I was feeling hungry enough to eat too.

"Hey, look!" said Ben, wiping his mouth and pointing to a man who was walking out of a gift shop for tourists. He was dressed in a dark green suit and hat that made him look like a train conductor and had a bunch of leaflets and a big badge that said INFORMATION OFFICER. "Let's ask him how to get to Greenwich!"

Pulling his Darth Vader mask on, Ben walked toward the man, his cloak floating behind him like a black sail. But before he could reach him, a large school group wearing bright red T-shirts and yellow baseball caps cut in front of Ben and surrounded the man with the leaflets. A tall woman holding up a yellow umbrella was shouting questions at the man, her mouth twitching and moving in every direction. We saw Ben trying to push his way through and failing, but then his Darth Vader mask started to nod. As the school group circled around the conductor man like a human solar system, the umbrella lady trying to get them under control, Ben came running back to us.

"Quick!" he said, lifting his mask so we could hear him better. "That school group is going to the pirate ship thing on the map! They asked the man how to get to Greenwich! Let's follow them!"

"That'sh s-super lucky, Aniyah!" said Travis, giving me a thumbs-up. I grinned back because I knew it was Mum helping us again. I could feel it. It felt like a giant wave rising up inside me and pushing me on.

"Thanks, Mum," I whispered out loud, knowing that she could hear me.

From behind us, the tall lady holding up the yellow umbrella was holding open the glass doors. "Keeeeds! You must-a stay-a with me!" she shouted, nodding quickly as she counted the bobbing heads that were flooding out past her. "You must not-a get-a-lost-a in this city! *Veloce! Veloce, per favore!*"

"What language is that?" asked Ben as we waited for the last of the group to exit the doors and began to follow them.

"I don't know," I said. "Spanish?"

"It's definitely not F-French," said Travis. "Maybe I-Italian?"

"I like Spanish!" said Noah, pulling on my hand and shaking his head so that it made his helmet wobble.

Following the school group without making it seem as if we were following them was trickier than we thought it would be. The teacher with the yellow umbrella and the two shorter teachers with her kept stopping to make sure everyone was together or to tell someone off. Whenever they stopped, we stopped too, and pretended to be pointing at things in the sky until they moved again.

We followed the group to an island of bus stops in the middle of two large roads; then we watched as they hurried toward one of the long bendy buses that look like red caterpillars and climbed on board.

"Come on!" I said, pulling on Noah's arm so that he would walk faster. As we got nearer to the wide-open doors of the bus, I could see right away that there wasn't a bus driver in the driver's seat yet—which meant they were probably on a break somewhere. Mum's star was making everything super easy for us!

I waved Travis and Ben on and helped Noah walk with me to the back seats. I could see the teacher with the yellow umbrella beeping lots of travel cards on a yellow machine, and I hoped no one would come and ask us for our cards too.

"Here he comesh!" whispered Travis as a large, round bus driver finally climbed into the driver's seat. We all waited to be asked where our tickets were, but he didn't look at anyone. He simply got into his seat, closed the doors with a hiss, cried out "All aboard!" and lurched the bus into motion.

"I love London!" whispered Ben, tapping me on the shoulder and making me love London again too.

But our love for London didn't last too long, because after just two stops, the bus came to a halt.

"What's going on?" asked Ben, squashing his face against the window.

"T-traffic," said Travis, shaking his head and shrugging his shoulders. "Just like on the c-coach!"

From somewhere outside, cars began to beep, and suddenly, the sound of sirens rang through the air.

Ben and Travis sat up straight and looked at me as I stared back at them. Was it the police? Had they found us? Were they the ones causing the traffic so that they could stop us?

We waited, the sirens getting louder and louder, until an ambulance flashed by.

"Phew!" whispered Ben, and we all relaxed again. "It's not for us!"

"Ladies and gentlemen, due to an incident up ahead, this bus is now on diversion," announced the bus driver over the loudspeaker. "If Greenwich Tunnel is *not* your final destination, please be sure to get off here."

The bus doors hissed open, but the teacher with the yellow umbrella and the class stayed on, so we did too.

"Come on!" I urged, willing the traffic to go away so we could move again. I was starting to get worried. I had no idea what time it was anymore or how far we were from the royal star hunters. I looked back up at the small black screen on the bus that usually told everyone the time and where they were, but it was broken and stayed blank.

After two more ambulances and a police car whizzed past, the bus finally jolted forward.

"Blinking blizzards!" said Ben. "About time!"

As we swerved in and out and down and up and around what felt like hundreds of streets, Noah fell into a deep sleep and Ben's mutterings became quieter and quieter, until he nodded off too. The teacher with the yellow umbrella was no longer shouting or trying to keep her class under control, because they had all fallen into a half daze like us. But finally, after what felt like half a day, the bus driver stopped the bus and shouted, *"Last stop! Everyone off!"*

"Cheeeeeeeldren! *Preparati! Preparati!* Bags and-a partners, *per favore*! Quickly!" cried the teacher, clapping her hands loudly and waking everyone up. She made her way to the doors, holding up her umbrella like a wand. As soon as the bus shuddered to a stop and everyone began to stream out of the doors, I shook Noah awake and pulled him to his feet. The long journey had made all of us so droopy and tired that my ankle had fallen asleep too. It sent out a horrible sharp pain as I woke it up, and made me bite my lip.

"Look over there," said Travis as we followed the school group to a pointy black sign on a pole that said GREENWICH FOOT TUNNEL 600 YARDS.

"Man!" said Ben, taking his mask off. "Finally! It's the tunnel on the map—and that must be the entrance!"

We watched as the school group made their way to a short, round, redbrick building with a strange domed roof, and disappeared inside it.

"Come get yer souvenirs fer the most famous river in the world!" called out a voice from near the doorway, as more people who had been on the bus with us walked past. "Ice creams and water fer just a pound-fifty—a mug's price fer yer if ever there was one!" As we got closer to the tunnel entrance, we saw a woman sitting on a stool in front of a small ice cream freezer decorated with lots of magnets and key rings.

"Niyah, can I have an ice cream?" asked Noah, taking off his helmet and pulling me toward the woman. "Pleeeeeeeeeeease!"

"We'll get one later, Noah! I promise," I said, trying to pull him back.

"No! I want one now, Niyah. . . . I said please!"

The woman watched us from her stool and smiled as Noah pulled us all closer to her.

"Well, hello there, little man!" she said kindly. "What would you like?"

"Strawberry and chocolate with ketchup sauce," said Noah, licking his lips.

"Ketchup?" asked the woman, frowning. "Ah! Yer mean strawberry sauce!" she said, holding up a red bottle and making Noah nod.

"Noah, not now," I said, pulling him away. "I said later!"

"Yeah, Noah, we'll g-get you a bigger one later!" promised Travis.

"No!" shouted Noah, his face turning red. "I don't want a bigger one! I want this one!"

I pulled on his arm harder as the woman kept frowning at us. She leaned forward on her stool and looked at me and Ben and Travis and Noah, as if she knew something about us that even we didn't know. From the top of her ice cream freezer, she snatched up a newspaper. "Hold on," said the woman. "Is your name Noah?"

I felt Ben and Travis freeze as Noah nodded. "Oh my . . . you're . . . you're them! The kids . . . from the paper!" cried the woman, her voice getting louder and louder.

For a second, we all looked at each other. Ben looked at me and I looked at Travis and Travis looked at the woman and Noah looked at the ice cream cart. Then suddenly, as if we had the exact same thought at the exact same moment, me and Travis and Ben yelled, *"Ruuuuuuun!"* and ran past the woman straight to the doors of the tunnel! I heard Ben's shoes squeak and thud and thump and Travis's rucksack jump and jangle as he picked Noah up on his back.

"Wait!" cried the woman, jumping up from her seat. *"Stop! Don't go looking for him! It's not saaaaaaaaaafe!"*

Running down the swirling staircase and trying to ignore the screams of my ankle, I looked over my shoulder. The woman wasn't following us—but something told me that was only because she was calling the police.

When we reached the bottom of the stairs, I stopped. I was feeling dizzy again and there were dots of lights in my eyes, which made the tunnel up ahead look as if it had been lit up by a giant disco ball.

"Come on, Aniyah!" shouted Ben, running back to grab my arm and pull me on. Even though my lungs and my chest and my ankle didn't want to, they followed him, and we all dived down into a narrow cave made of glimmering white tiles and headed under London's ground just as fast as our breaths and feet would let us.

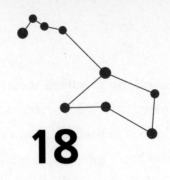

18

Starboard

"Is she . . . behind us?" panted Ben, wiping his face with his sleeves.

Travis shook his head.

"Good!" said Ben, stopping to hold his sides and bend over. "I can't . . . run . . . any . . . more!"

"Me . . . neither!" I said, leaning my back and head against one of the curvy walls and sitting down. We had run as hard and as fast as we could for what must have been half the tunnel, and I couldn't take another step. My head was pounding and my face felt as if it was on fire. I took off my tiger hood and wished the tunnel had some fresh air to help cool me down.

Travis slipped Noah down from his back and began to wheeze as if something was stuck in his throat. He held his hand out to Ben, who stared at it for a few seconds before crying, "Oh! Water!" and handing us our bottles. We all fell silent as we gulped down what we had left.

Noah rubbed his eyes and came and buried his head into my stomach angrily. He wanted me to know he wasn't happy and wasn't talking to me anymore.

Ben pointed up ahead. "So where's the end?" he asked, frowning.

Blinking my eyes to make the floating spots go away, I looked the way Ben was pointing. The curved white-tiled walls and the long yellow ceiling lights of the tunnel went on for so long that it looked as if there wasn't any light at the end to try to get to.

"Come on," wheezed Travis as he splashed the last few drops of his water over his face. "Let's keep going! She m-might—shtill be coming!"

Giving Noah my trick-or-treat sweet bag to say sorry and to make him forget about the ice cream, I tried to take his hand and start running again.

But my bad ankle couldn't touch the ground for more than a few quick seconds anymore. I bit my lip and tried to hop a few steps to show Ben and Travis I was OK, but I couldn't.

"Here," said Ben, placing one of my arms around his neck as Travis came and pulled the other one around his.

"We n-need to go to the h-hospital," Travis said, looking at me sadly.

I shook my head as I began to hop. "Not until I make them give Mum's star the right name," I said, gripping on to Travis's and Ben's necks more tightly. They nodded back, and I knew it was a promise from them that they wouldn't make me give up. Not when we were nearly there.

As Noah loudly ate his way through what was left of my treats bag and skipped next to Travis's leg, the rest of us walked on through the tunnel in silence. Once we caught up with the school group we had gotten on the bus with, we slowed down so that we were just a few steps behind them. They were making so much noise it seemed as if the tunnel was filled with a million people—which was good because it meant people walking in the opposite direction didn't notice us as much. But we still got lots of stares, especially whenever Noah decided it was funny to grab hold of my tiger tail and roar.

But it didn't matter. All that mattered was getting to the end of the tunnel and making it to the star hunters without getting caught—by the ice cream woman or anyone else. I could tell Ben and Travis were thinking the same thing, because they had the same kinds of frowns on their faces as I did.

Hopping on a hurt foot through a never-ending tunnel started to do funny things to my brain. It made me wonder about a million different things. Like about what Eddie and Kwan from school were doing and if Dad had seen me and Noah in the news flash today and had guessed that the new star in the sky was Mum's heart. And about the crumpets that Mum used to make us for special breakfasts, and how they always looked like a yellow moon dotted with craters and covered in golden butter. And then why me hurting my ankle might be a good thing, because if I went to the hospital and had to stay there, then Noah could stay with me and we could tell the doctors to tell Dad to come and get us, and tell Mrs. Iwuchukwu to adopt Ben and Travis before they got any taller. There was so much to do after Mum's star got the right name, and I had to make it all happen.

"Hey!" said Travis. "Can you see that? I think I see something!"

Ben and I narrowed our eyes to try to see better. There, far ahead, was a glowing circle of light that wasn't a ceiling light.

"Thank my giddy uncles," said Ben from under his mask. "Finally! We're near the end!"

We walked and hopped faster now, with Noah swooping around us pretending to be an airplane. As the gap between the ceiling lights and the floor got bigger and the glowing light became stronger, a large white line painted on the floor met our feet. Written along the top of it in capital letters were the words:

WELCOME TO GREENWICH: WHERE TIME MEETS SPACE

It was the best finish line I had ever seen. We all crossed over it in silence as the school group up ahead came to a stop.

"Let's get the lift with them this time!" said Ben, looking worriedly at my ankle.

"We have to be c-careful," said Travis. "Up there." He pointed upward to make sure we understood. "D-don't let go of us, Aniyah—we might need to walk f-fasht."

We waited for the large metal lift to arrive, then squeezed ourselves in between the students and the woman with the yellow umbrella and an old couple who were talking in a loud American accent.

"*Aniyah!* We're going to space!" exclaimed Noah happily as he felt the lift take off beneath our feet. He stood with his nose pressed against the crisscrossed metal grilles and watched the ground below fall away. After a few minutes, the lift stopped with a loud clang and the doors skidded open. As the class around us began to shuffle out, I looked up and saw someone standing on tiptoes, looking all around. It was the ice cream woman—and next to her were two policemen!

"Duck!" I whispered, pulling Ben and Travis down by the elbows and signaling at them to hide behind the school group and stay as far away from the woman as possible. Travis pulled Noah closer to him and put a finger to his lips to warn him to be silent. Bending down as low as we could, we left the lift and made our way outside, using the students as our shields. We were instantly surrounded by hundreds of people walking and taking pictures and pointing at things. The woman and the policemen were only a few short steps away, but they were still peering into the lift searchingly.

"There!" whispered Travis as he waved us in the direction of a large van selling cupcakes and cotton candy right next to the tunnel building.

We hid behind the van and waited to make sure we were still safe.

"I can literally taste my heartbeat right now," whispered Ben.

"That was close," I said as we watched one of the policemen talking into his walkie-talkie while the woman shrugged. Then they all walked into the tunnel building and looked down the stairs.

"Niyah, look—there's a pirate ship!" said Noah, pulling on my arm and running out to the middle of the busy pavement.

"That's cool!" said Ben as we followed Noah out and looked up. We couldn't see the woman or the policemen at all anymore, so it seemed like we were safe.

We all stood staring up at one of the largest, shiniest, most piratey pirate ships I had ever seen. It looked as if it was made up of a thousand needles trying to pierce the sky, all connected by a giant spiderweb. And what made the ship feel even more special was that it was sitting on top of a large diamond made of glass, which sparkled like the sea whenever the sun shone on it.

Standing on one leg, I took out my Royal Observatory souvenir guide from my bag.

"Look, we're here," I said, pointing to the small cartoon of the *Cutty Sark,* which looked exactly like our pirate ship. "And we need to go this way—to here." I walked my fingers from the ship, to the label that said "Greenwich Market," across the trees, and finally to the image of the telescope.

From somewhere far away, a bell began to ring.

Dong.

Dong.

Dong.

Dong.

"Is it four o'clock already?" I asked, feeling shocked. The traffic jams and the diversions and my ankle had all made us so late!

Ben nodded. "Must be."

"Let's go, then," I said firmly. And with a nod, we headed off toward the market, ready for whatever time and space might do to us.

19

Crossing the
Thin Black Line

"Excuse me, sir, but which way is it to the star hunters' house?" asked Ben as he stuck another handful of steaming hot chips into his mouth. The smells of the market had made all our mouths water, so Travis spent more of his money on a large packet of vinegar-drenched chips for us to share while we walked.

The old man looked down at Ben with a frown.

"The star what now?" he asked.

"Sorry, sir, he means the Royal Observatory," I said, grinning at Ben.

"Oh! Well, that's that way!" said the man, trying to stop his dog from pulling him away, and pointing to a long road that sloped upward. "Just follow that road to the end, then it's the park, and straight up the hill." The man's gray eyebrows squeezed together. He looked at all of us through his half-moon glasses, then glanced at his watch and then back at us. "But it's closing early for a special event—and it's past four-thirty now, so you won't get in."

"Oh, we'll get in!" said Ben, giving the old man such a huge smile that it made him take a step back. "Our dad works there! Thanks!"

The old man scratched his head and looked confused, but he let his dog pull him away.

"He'll be thinking about that one for *hours*," said Ben.

"G-good one," Travis said with a grin as Noah jumped up to take some more chips.

"Our *dad* . . . ?" said Ben as he saw me frowning. "'Cause we *definitely* all look like we'd have the *same* dad!"

"Oh!" I said, feeling stupid. I had been busy thinking about what the old man had said—that the observatory would be closing soon and that we wouldn't be able to get in. We hadn't planned for what we needed to do *after* we reached the observatory. What if, after all this, we couldn't get in?

We began to walk and hop-walk and piggyback-ride in the direction the man had pointed out to us, up the long sloping road toward the park. The sky was starting to get darker, as the sun had left for the night, and the only noises we could hear were people laughing and drinking from inside brightly lit pubs and restaurants.

"Where are we now?" asked Ben.

"C-can't be far," said Travis as the top of the road came into sight. Up ahead was a long row of tall black gates decorated with golden curls. Two of the biggest gates were wide open, and two large men dressed in long black coats with wires coming out of their ears were standing next to a red rope that stopped anyone from going in. Behind them, far away in the distance and on top of a hill, there it was! A large dome and a brick house, lit up with yellow and blue lights . . . the Royal Observatory. We were so close!

An extra-long and extra-shiny black car slowly drove past us. We watched as it stopped at the open gates, and one of the large men walked up to the back window. A white glove with a huge diamond ring on it poked out and showed him a card. The man nodded, making the second man take the red rope down to let the car in.

"They musht be here for the party," whispered Travis.

"Yeah, and they're undercover police," said Ben knowingly. "We'd better not get seen by them! Look, there's a signboard over there. Let's go and see if it says anything."

We followed Ben to a large glass case in front of the gates. Inside it was a colorful green map, which had an arrow saying YOU ARE HERE, and lots of little cards written in different handwriting, asking things like HAVE YOU SEEN THIS DOG? and LOOKING FOR YOUR SOUL MATE? In the middle of all of them was a poster filled with shining fireworks and sparkling stars. And written in golden letters were the words:

TONIGHT!
THE KRONOS ANNUAL GALA
Celebrating 250 Years of Keeping the World's Time
Please note: All sections of the Royal Observatory and Planetarium will be closed to visitors from 16:00.

"Aw, man! It's closed already!" whispered Ben, looking over his shoulder at the two men as if they were to blame.

Pushing my face through the gap between two railings, I looked up to the house. We were so close. We had to get in . . . we just had to! We couldn't have come all this way and then not make it inside. I couldn't let Mum's star wander the skies forever with the wrong name just because of some silly gates!

I stretched my hands out, wishing I could reach the house somehow or touch the royal telescope. It all felt so near. I looked at my arms and hands stretched out in front of me, and suddenly had an idea!

"Come on," I said, pulling Ben's and Travis's arms. "I

think I know how we can all get in. We just have to make sure no one sees us!"

Ben and Travis looked confused as I began to hop-walk away from where the two undercover-spy men were standing, and followed the railings along the road. We carried on walking until the house and restaurants and voices and lights and trees had disappeared, and the railing met a brick wall. There was nowhere else to go, and there was no one around to see us.

"Here," I said, taking off my rucksack. "We can get in here!"

"Get in where?" asked Ben.

"Watch!" I said. And breathing out just as much as I could and sucking in my stomach, I grabbed my tiger tail and went up to two of the iron bars. Sticking one leg between them, and then following my leg with an arm, I gradually squeezed the rest of my body through. Turning my face to the side, I closed my eyes as the corners of the metal scraped against my cheeks. I felt squashed and as if I might not be able to breathe, but it only lasted for a second and then—pop!—I was in. I was on the other side of the gates!

"See!" I said, rubbing my face so that it felt normal again. "Easy!"

Ben lined himself up against the railings to see if he

would fit. "But . . . my hair . . . ," he muttered, touching it, as if squeezing through the railings might make it all fall out.

"Noah firsht," said Travis, pushing him forward.

"Noah, come on! Come here," I whispered, pulling him toward the railings. Noah gave me his arms and let me pull him through, his space helmet crashing into the railings and toppling off as he popped through. Travis slid it through the railings, along with my rucksack, and then he slid through too. In the dark, his skeleton suit was beginning to glow a luminous white green.

"Oh man! I'm not gonna fit," said Ben, touching his hair again.

"Yes you will," I said. "You just have to breathe out— like I did!"

"Come on, B-Ben!" said Travis. "We'll help with the hair!"

"Fine. I mean . . . I can tell it isn't going to work, but you can't say I didn't try," muttered Ben as he grabbed a railing and took a deep breath in. Squeezing through half his face and then a leg and then his chest, he held out a hand. "I'm stuck! I'm stuck!" Noah started to giggle as he watched me and Travis grab Ben's arm and pull as hard as we could. A river of sweets fell out of Ben's pocket as we tried to tug his body through.

"*Owwwwwwww!*" shouted Ben. "Jiminy buckets! Why are these railings so close together? I'm gonna die!"

"Shhhhhh!" I warned as I pulled even harder.

"Wait! My hair! My hair!" he shrieked as his face squashed its way past the railings.

"F-forget the hair and breathe out more!" ordered Travis.

"*Owwwwwwww!*" shouted Ben again as we pulled on his arm until it felt as if it might come off. But his chest was beginning to move toward us and his face was nearly all the way through and then—with a pop!—Ben was on the same side of the gates as us.

"That hurt!" he gasped as he checked to see if he was still in one piece. "I thought I was going to die—that would have been so embarrassing! Wait!" Quickly touching his hair, he asked, "Is it OK?" Travis and me looked at each other, trying not to laugh. Ben's perfectly round circle of hair had now become a slightly wonky, fluffy rectangle.

Noah giggled as Ben frowned.

"G-good idea about the railings, Aniyah!" said Travis as he came to help me walk on.

"Yeah," said Ben. "Even if it did nearly k—"

"Shhhh!" I whispered, pulling Noah close to me.

I could hear a quiet rustling in the grass getting closer and louder.

We all stood like strangely shaped tree statues and waited, feeling scared.

"*Aaaaaaaaaaaaaagggggggggggggh! Raaaaaaaaaaaaaaats!*" shouted Ben, pointing behind me and running off as fast as he could into the trees.

My heart beating in my ears, I slowly looked over my shoulder. A furry gray face with a bushy tail popped up with a chocolate peanut held between its paws. It must have smelled all the sweets that had dropped out of Ben's pockets and come to investigate.

"It's only squirrels," I shouted, letting out the breath I had been holding and beginning to laugh. "Ben! Stop! It's OK," I called out to him.

"I'm gonna *kill* him," said Travis, putting his hand where his heart was and shaking his head.

As Ben came running back to us, I took Noah's hand and looked up ahead. Through the trees in front of us, I could see a field and more trees and a long winding road. Even though we were on the other side of the gates now, the dome of the observatory was still a long way away. But in the air, I could hear the sound of music and distant voices, all telling us that the biggest competition in the galaxy was coming to an end, and that this was my last chance to help Mum's star and give her back the name she was born with.

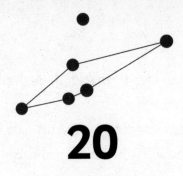

20

The Nut Job

"I wonder how many people entered the competition," said Ben as he helped me hop over another big branch and past another long line of trees.

"P-probably millionsh and millionsh," said Travis as he bounced Noah on his back and tried to stop himself from being strangled at the same time. "But it doesn't change the f-fact that you ran away f-from a s-squirrel!"

"They're *like* rats!" argued Ben. "Just . . . fluffier!"

From somewhere far behind, we heard the same clock bell from an hour ago begin to ring again.

Dong.

Dong.

Dong.

Dong.

Dong.

It was five o'clock already! Which meant we now had less than two hours to get up the hill to the star hunters and stop them from giving Mum's star the wrong name.

Hearing the bell ring made all of us try to hurry. But it was getting harder to walk through the forest quickly. The sky was completely dark now and the bushes and trees had started to look almost as black as the sky. I could hear Travis tripping and slipping and stumbling and felt Ben's grip on my arm tighten as he tried to help me without falling over sticks and branches and slippery bits of mud himself.

We walked on and on as the land sloped up and up. Noah began to make whining noises and we all began to breathe more heavily and walk more slowly.

"Finally," said Ben as we came to a stop behind a giant tree trunk. "We're here!"

We all crouched behind the giant tree and looked around. There were no more trees in front of us, and no more muddy fields. There was only a long row of empty black cars, all perfectly parked in a grid, the same way that Noah parked his toy cars whenever he was pretending they were in a traffic jam. On the other side of the road and behind the cars was a large wall surrounding a huge red-bricked building with a giant metal telescope poking out from the ground in front of it. Six black bowls on extra-tall sticks were flickering with fire, and in front of them was an open gate leading to some stairs. A big bulky man in a black coat and a woman wearing a suit were waiting by the gates. Both of them had curly wires coming out of their ears, just like the ones we had seen on the undercover guards at the bottom of the hill.

I stared at the sign, which glowed out at us from the wall in front like a giant invitation made out of mirrors. It read WELCOME TO ROYAL OBSERVATORY GREENWICH AND THE PETER HARRISON PLANETARIUM.

"How are we going to get in?" asked Ben as we hid behind the tree trunk and watched the flames of the fires swirl about in the wind.

"I don't know," I said, feeling worried. I had never thought about the star hunters being protected by bowls of fire and security guards. All the pictures I had seen in books about them had made it seem like they lived in libraries and were always ready to help anyone who wanted to find something out about space. They would have to help us if we found a way past the guards—wouldn't they?

I shook the question away and looked at Noah, who was nearly asleep on Travis's back. "What if we pretend that our parents are inside? And Noah can pretend-cry?"

Travis shook his head. "They'll p-probably ask us f-for n-names and check their l-list and a-arrest ush if we g-get it wrong."

We all decided Travis was right and tried to think of something else.

After another minute, just as Noah began to snore lightly, Travis suddenly turned around excitedly. "W-wait a minute! I think I've g-got it!" ·

"What?" Ben and I asked together.

Travis pointed to the cars in front of us. "We use them!"

"Er . . . the cars?" asked Ben, frowning.

Travis nodded. "Yeah! Because what do c-cars have?" he asked us.

Ben shrugged. "Wheels?"

Travis shook his head and, giving Ben a nudge with his elbow, said, "No . . . alarms!"

Ben's eyebrows slowly straightened and then curved upward.

"Travis! You're a *genius*!" he cried, shaking Travis by the arms as if they were glow sticks he was trying to light. "But how?"

"Alarms?" I asked, trying to understand what they were both talking about.

"The s-sweets!" said Travis. "From our t-treat bagsh?"

Ben grabbed his rucksack, pulled out what was left of the treat bags, and held them up like trophies. Ben's was empty, Noah's was nearly finished and he'd eaten half of mine too, but Travis's hadn't even been opened yet.

"P-perfect!" said Travis. He took one bag from Ben and poured the contents into his trouser pockets, then watched as Ben did the same with the other bags.

"What are you going to do?" I asked, feeling more confused than ever.

"We're going to u-use them—for a trick!" Travis grinned.

"Yeah," said Ben. "A trick that's going to get all of us inside that gate! All we need is to cause a little alarm. Get it? *Cause* an *alarm*?"

I carried on frowning. But suddenly, I understood!

"That's brilliant!" I cried, clapping my hands over my mouth in case I had shouted too loudly. But the security guards on the other side of the road didn't look as if they had heard anything.

"We'll go set them off," said Ben, putting his mask back on. "Just be ready to run in, OK?"

I nodded.

"Get ready!" ordered Travis as he slipped Noah off his back. I took Noah's arms and tried to make him stand up. But he barely opened his eyes and groaned at me instead.

"Shhhhhhh!" warned Travis as we all poked our heads out from the tree and looked at the guards across the road. One of them had stopped marching up and down and was looking around suspiciously. But after a few seconds, he went back to walking around again.

"OK," said Travis as I pulled Noah to his feet again. "Here—here we go."

Ben nodded, biting his bottom lip so hard that it disappeared into his mouth.

I nodded too. But I was starting to feel so nervous that I didn't know if it was really a nod or just my neck shivering.

"OK . . . you g-go left, and I'll go r-right, and we'll m-meet at the gates!" ordered Travis.

Ben gave a thumbs-up and checked his pockets to make sure all the sweets were still there.

Pulling Noah behind me, I crept out from behind the tree and we quickly made our way to the car closest to us. Crouching low next to one of its doors, I put a finger to my lips and signaled to Noah to stay silent. He put a finger to his lips too, copying me and looking serious and more awake.

I watched as Ben and Travis both receded into the dark, Travis's glow-in-the dark skeleton taking longer to disappear. I waited and listened and tried to keep Noah standing up . . . until finally I heard it—a sound like hailstones falling from a distant part of the sky! Travis and Ben were throwing the sweets high into the air so that they landed on the roofs of the cars, making the metal ping gently.

Then everything went silent again.

For a few seconds, I sat and waited, feeling sick. What

if it hadn't worked? What if sweets weren't heavy enough to set the alarms off? But then, like a siren coming to life, a light started to flash and the sound of a car alarm split the night. And then another . . . and another!

Ney-neeeeeeere!

Peeee-paaaaaw!

Oooo-noooooooo!

"What the blazes—?" cried one of the security guards, rushing past us to the left, where the sounds were coming from.

Then, as if calling out to the first group of noises, new alarms began to sound from the opposite side.

Gyooooowng!

Heeeeee-hooooooo!

No-waaaaaaaaay!

Rushing back to my side, his hair sticking up as if in excitement, Travis grabbed my arm. We watched the second security guard leave the gate and run toward the second lot of cars on our right. Almost instantly, Ben appeared out of the shadows, looking nervous but happy.

"Quick," he said, pointing ahead. The trick had worked! The gates of the planetarium were wide open, and there was no one to stop us from going inside!

Grabbing each other's arms, we edged to the other side

of the car and checked to our left and right. There was no sign of the guards, but two of the car alarms had already stopped screaming.

"Go!" whispered Travis as he pushed himself up, and he began sprinting as hard and as fast as he could toward the gates, pulling me and Noah and Ben along behind him.

As we stumbled across the road, past the gates and onto the thick red carpet that led the way up the steps and to the planetarium doors, we heard another two car alarms come to life behind us. Followed by another. And another!

"Who's throwing more sweets?" whispered Ben as we all looked at each other in confusion.

"Come on—let's see!" Travis waved us on.

When he reached the top, just a few paces ahead, Travis turned away from the entrance and toward the wall over-looking the car park instead. Following him, we all came to a stop, our mouths falling open at what we saw.

Because there below us, running up and down on the shiny black roofs of all the cars, and making more alarms go off, was a whole army of fluffy gray squirrels, all run-ning after the chocolate-covered nuts that Ben and Travis had thrown up into the air for them!

And chasing them, with their coats flapping in the wind and their faces all red and hot and sweaty, were the two security guards, swearing at them loudly and trying to shoo them away.

"Travis, I think this could be your best trick yet," said Ben, with a proud smile on his face.

"Not just that," I exclaimed as a laugh made its way to my throat, "this is the best trick ever played, in the whole history of the galaxy!"

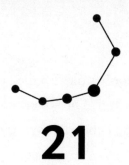

21

The Biggest Star in Hollywood

"Time to f-find the star huntersh!" said Travis as he held out his hand to Noah, who was staring openmouthed at the squirrels as if they were his own personal Christmas presents.

Turning toward the big red building that had been waiting behind us, all of us became quiet again, except for Noah.

"I hope we don't have to get past any more guards," said Ben as we pressed our noses up against the glass doors and looked through them. We could see it was dark inside, but on all the walls were moving pictures of stars and planets and a clock with its hands moving both backward and forward and the words KRONOS WATCHES: TIME'S OWN MASTERPIECE flashing up in big white writing every few seconds. There was no one inside.

Gripping the door handle, I pulled open the door, hoping that it wasn't locked. The sound of distant talking and then people clapping echoed across the room from somewhere downstairs.

We stepped inside together and headed toward the spiral staircase in the center of the huge room. A board that said KRONOS ANNUAL GALA DINNER, with an arrow pointing downward, stood on the top step, next to a thick red rope hooked onto two golden sticks.

"Come on," I said. "Let's go down!"

I led the way, hopping as fast as I could, wondering what we would find when we reached the bottom, and how I was going to make everyone listen to me about Mum's star. I didn't know what the time was anymore, but I knew we didn't have much of it left.

Ducking under the rope, we quietly made our way down the circling stairs. The lower we went, the darker it became, and the tighter I held Noah's hand. Another sign, this time saying KRONOS GALA DINNER STRAIGHT AHEAD, pointed to a long corridor. It was almost completely dark, but as we walked through it, pictures of planets and comets and black holes lit up and shone out from the walls and even the ceiling. The sound of music and laughter came out in spirals from the next room.

"Look!" shouted Noah as a picture flashed up on a

large black screen at the end of the corridor. It was of a swirling mass of white-pink light, and showed two long tornado shapes squeezing it from above and below into a smaller and smaller ball, until, without warning, it suddenly exploded into a burst of blue silver. The words *How a Star Is Born* appeared and, after three seconds, faded into darkness. I stared at our shadows reflected in the screen, and looked down at Noah. I never knew what it looked like when new stars were born, but now everything made sense. I wanted to tell Noah that I knew now why the crack we had felt in our chests had hurt so much, and why the explosion we had heard the night Mum disappeared had been so loud. Mum's heart had gone through such a big change! And even though it made her even more beautiful than she already was, and meant that she could live for millions of years, it still looked painful and lonely.

"Aniyah?"

I felt a hand tap my shoulder and knew it was Travis trying to make me hurry up. But even though I wanted to turn away, I couldn't. Seeing how Mum's heart might have been changed into a star had turned my insides into electricity and stone.

A huge round of applause vibrated all around us, making the double doors near us shake. The sound raced through me and forced me to turn around. Gulping down the sticky ball in my throat, I led Ben and Travis and Noah to the end of the star-filled room.

Silently, I pushed open one of the doors a tiny crack so we could see what was happening.

Inside, the room was filled with lots of round tables covered with tall candles and flowers. Around the tables were men dressed in shiny black suits with bow ties and white shirts that made them look like penguins, and women wearing ball gowns of every color. Some of them were wearing large diamonds on their necks and ears and even in their hair, as if they were in a competition to see who could be the shiniest. And by our door and all along the sides of the room were even more people holding large cameras that clicked and flashed and filled the air with strange whirring noises.

As our heads sneaked further and further through the door, I noticed that everyone in the room was looking and whispering and clicking and flashing at a woman walking up to a big glass stage right at the end of the room. Even though she didn't have diamonds in her hair or in her ears like all the other women, and her ball gown wasn't even a bit shiny, she looked as if she might be the most beautiful woman in the world. Her skin was shining and her hair was black and wavy and fell in curls around her face. Her black dress floated all the way down to the floor, around her neck she was wearing the whitest pearls I had ever seen, and just like Mrs. Iwuchukwu, she had glitter all around her eyes.

"Buckets of bouncing balls . . . that's—that's . . ." Ben fell silent and began poking me and Travis in the arms a hundred times a second. "It's the actress from all the super-hero films! Audrey . . . something!"

"Yeah, I know!" said Travis, turning red and suddenly looking shy. "She'sh the b-biggest shtar in Hollywood!"

We watched as the woman named Audrey Something stood up behind a glass column and looked around the room. Everyone waited in silence, as if what she was about to say might be the most important thing their ears might ever hear.

"Ladies and gentlemen, esteemed patrons, beneficia-ries, timekeepers, and astronomers! I am honored to be here today as the new face of Kronos Watches."

A huge round of applause shook the room and she gave a small bow with her head, then continued to speak.

"I am even more honored to be standing here today, at the place where modern time was born, and where the human desire to learn all that it can of the worlds contained within our galaxies continues to grow. I have learned so much in my role as an ambassador for Kronos Enterprise and Foundation, and I look forward greatly to meeting you all.

"But now," she continued. "It gives me great pleasure to open tonight's gala with the naming of a new phenomenon in our skies! As you know, three days ago the astronomers of the Royal Observatory were the first to spot the now-famous star that has transcended the laws of physics. The first star to not only show itself to the naked eye, but journey closer to us than any star in our galaxy!"

Another round of applause exploded across the room, making my ears turn red. Ben and Travis turned around and gave me a grin, as if they were proud of Mum too.

"In the seventy-two hours since the launch of the global competition to help name this new star, I am pleased to inform you that over seventeen million names were submitted by people from every corner of our world, and at precisely one minute past twelve this morning, a winning name was selected by our computers!"

A cheer went up across the room that was so big it made the floors shake as if an earthquake was happening.

"Seventeen million . . . ," whispered Ben, his mouth falling open.

I continued watching as a short man with gray spiky hair and dressed in a suit joined Audrey Something onstage.

"Aniyah!" whispered Travis, nudging me. "Look! He's got the name! We're just in time."

I had seen the large golden envelope the man was holding in his hands, but I felt my hands and feet turning cold and I couldn't move. . . .

"Since its selection, the name has been sealed in an envelope and guarded by the lovely Mr. Alex Withers here. And in just thirty short seconds, we will be announcing our new star's new name!" With a bow, Mr. Withers handed Miss Audrey the envelope and everyone began clapping again.

Feeling my head begin to pound and my heartbeat in my mouth, I told my hands and feet to move. But they wouldn't listen. Time was running out and the envelope was now in Audrey Something's hands and Mum was about to be called the wrong name and I still couldn't move!

"On behalf of Kronos Watches and Royal Observatory Greenwich, I would like to thank everyone who submitted a name—and everyone here tonight, for being present to witness this moment in history."

With another clap of her hands, Miss Audrey bowed, and an invisible drum began to beat. The lights switched off, the whole room darkened, and a cinema screen behind the stage switched on, flashing out giant white numbers.

10 . . . 9 . . . 8 . . . 7 . . .

Time slowed down, the thumping in my mouth grew, and I felt my body go ice-cold.

"Aniyah!" hissed Ben. I heard him, but it was like he was speaking to me through a wall of jelly, which made his voice slow and wobbly.

6 . . . 5 . . . 4 . . .

Then, from the corner of my eye, I saw a shadow moving behind us. Over Ben's and Travis's shoulders was a large bald man running down the dark corridor of stars toward us. And I could see the curl of a wire from one of his ears.

"*Oi!*" he shouted as he spotted us.

"*No!*" I cried out, unfreezing myself and pushing open the doors in front of me all the way. I heard the man shouting behind me, but now that I was moving, I couldn't stop.

Bursting into the large dark room with a bang, I tried to run across the room to reach the golden envelope. But I had forgotten that my ankle wasn't working and that I was still wearing a tiger costume, because just as I reached the stage, I suddenly felt something long and thin wrap around my legs and a sharp and blinding crack shatter through my foot. I had tripped up over my tiger tail and was tumbling through the air as if I was flying through space. As I fell forward with a deafening crash, all I could hear were gasps and the floating sound of dresses being swished and chairs being scraped back against the floor. A ripple of "Oh mys!" swept all around me as I lay still, with my head buried in my arms. I wanted to get up. I wanted to say something and show everyone I was OK. But I wasn't sure if I could. Instead, I could feel my shoulders shaking and my legs lying like dead fish underneath me, wrapped in the treacherous tiger tail.

"Well now," said a voice, which was getting nearer to my ears as the lights of the room got stronger. "What do we have here?"

I felt a pair of hands put themselves on my arms and lift me up.

"Please!" I heard my voice say. "You can't open the envelope! You can't give my mum's star the wrong name! You can't!"

Keeping my eyes tightly shut and my head down so that my hair covered my face, I stayed still. I didn't want to see Travis or Ben or Noah because I knew I had let them down and I didn't want anyone to see me either. Then I sensed footsteps and felt small fingers pulling on my hair and shaking my arms, and I heard Noah's voice crying, "Niyah! Niyah!"

One of the strong hands left my shoulders and gently pushed my hair away from my face. I opened my eyes and looked up. A pair of wide brown-green eyes surrounded by silvery-white glitter was staring at me.

"Hello there," she said. "My name's Audrey. What's yours?"

And as if they couldn't wait another second, hundreds of cameras began to whiz and click and flash like streaks of lightning as the biggest star in Hollywood parted her bright red lips and smiled at me.

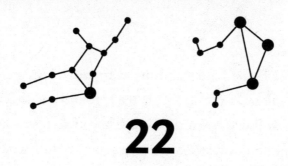

22

The Thief Who Stole a Life

Sitting up, I looked toward the stage and the cinema screen to check if the countdown had stopped. But there were too many people bending over me and staring for me to see a thing.

"Honey, what's your name?" asked Miss Audrey again, looking into my eyes as if I was the only person in the whole room.

I wiped my eyes and mumbled, "Aniyah."

"That's a beautiful name," she said. "Now, how about we unwrap that rather gorgeous tail from around your feet, and get you up, OK?"

I nodded and kept my head low. "Everyone, please," said Miss Audrey, putting her hands out. "Let's give the child a little space now."

As she helped me stand up, with Noah trying to help too by pulling on my arm, I glanced around and saw Travis and Ben halfway down the aisle. They looked shocked, as if they couldn't believe the biggest star in Hollywood was talking to me. I tried to say sorry to them with my eyes for embarrassing them and not stopping the countdown sooner, but I didn't know if they saw it.

"There," Miss Audrey said as she propped me up onto my feet. "How are you feeling?"

I wiped my eyes again and said, "OK," even though my knees felt sore and my elbows had skidded on the floor and I was pretty sure my ankle was broken now.

"Ah . . . you've hurt your leg there," said Miss Audrey, seeing me stand only on my good leg. She put her arm around me to help me stay steady. "And your face too," she added, frowning.

"Out of my way, please! Sir, ma'am! Out of my way!" The large bald man with the wire in his ear who'd been chasing us pushed his way through the crowds like an angry bulldozer until he reached me and Noah. "Ma'am, these kids have to come with me! They're trespassers."

"Is that so?" asked another voice from behind my head.

"Yes. We just saw CCTV footage of them breaking into the grounds through the side gates and, er . . . using some squirrels to cause a diversion to get in here," reported the guard.

I could feel Miss Audrey's eyes looking at me as Travis and Ben slowly stepped forward to stand beside me. Noah was staring up at the bald man and, realizing we were in trouble, began to hiccup so loudly that I was sure it was hurting his chest.

The bald man took a step forward and reached out as if he was going to grab my arm. This was it—I was going to go to jail. Probably forever. And this was even before everyone knew I had made us all run away from Mrs. Iwuchukwu's house and stolen her bike.

"Oh, don't be silly, Frank," said the voice behind my head again, as its owner came and stood next to Miss Audrey. "Tell your team not to go on the warpath over some kids! I'll sort it out!"

I looked up and, through the thick sheet of tears that was covering my eyes, saw a woman with long black hair, and a very long face with round brown eyes and sparkling glasses. She looked familiar, but I didn't know why.

"Sorry, ma'am," the bald man called Frank said, shaking his head. "It's procedure."

"They're just children," said Miss Audrey, smiling at Noah and giving his face a squeeze with her fingers. Noah looked at her shyly and hiccuped again, but more quietly this time.

"Children that broke in, ma'am," said Frank, his face and chest puffing up like a blowfish.

"Oh, come on!" cried a man from the audience, making lots more voices around me mutter and grumble and shake their heads.

"Why don't we get them inside the dome and hear what they have to say?" asked Mr. Withers, who now appeared behind Frank. "Professor Grewal?"

I gasped as the woman nodded. She was the star hunter from the news too! Forgetting that I was about to be arrested and that I couldn't feel my legs anymore, I blurted out, "Professor Grewal! You're a star hunter! You *have* to help my mum! Please! Please can you help her?"

Frowning at me, Professor Grewal asked, "What do you mean, Aniyah? How does your mum need help?"

"*She's* the star. It's her heart—you see?" I asked, hoping she would understand me. "Please, you can't give her the wrong name! You can't give her the one the computers chose. Please . . ."

All around me, I heard more whispers and gasps as Professor Grewal and Audrey Something both looked at each other and had a secret conversation with their eyes.

"You *have* to help!" shouted Ben, as if he couldn't be

quiet any longer. "We've been trying to get to you all night and all day. And we nearly even got killed!" he finished as Travis stared openmouthed and nodded along.

Unable to stand any longer, I felt my knees begin to wobble. Miss Audrey caught my arms and, shouting, "Make way, please!" led me over to a chair that a worried-looking man in a penguin suit was sitting in.

"Sir?" asked Miss Audrey, making the man jump up and offer the chair to me.

As I sat down, I felt a wave of bodies pressing down on me. There were so many eyes and faces and shining jewels looking at me that it felt as if the whole room was leaning in and trying to see what was going on.

"Kids, come here, please," ordered Professor Grewal, motioning to Ben and Travis to come and sit next to me, but on the floor. Smiling at us, she asked Ben and Noah and Travis what their names were, and then asked me what a "star hunter" was and why I needed one to help me. Wanting her to know everything, we all began to answer at once.

"My mum's heart became a star last week and she's the one you saw and launched the competition about and we knew we needed to get to the star hunters here so that you'd know the truth and wouldn't call her the wrong name!"

"We had to come find you," said Ben.

"So that you d-don't get her name wrong!" added Travis as Noah gave a loud "Hic!" and added, "Mum's star is the biggest."

"I'm a star hunter too, so that's how I know it's her star!" I explained, looking at Professor Grewal.

"So we had to r-run away to g-get here on time!"

"That's how we hurt ourselves!"

"But I didn't mean to get anyone in trouble!"

"Hic!"

"Everyone . . . stop a moment, please!" said Mr. Withers, putting his hands up. Everyone in the whole room watched as he came over to me, kneeled down, and asked, "Aniyah. Do you mean to say that you think—sorry—that you believe your mum's heart is the star we're celebrating tonight?"

I nodded as Miss Audrey gasped and went, "Oh!"

"I see . . . and why do you think that?" carried on Mr. Withers, his warm brown eyes and gray-brown beard both looking up at me.

I stayed silent, because I had never told anyone about the crash I had felt or the explosion I had heard. But before I could say anything, Noah clapped his hands and said, "Because she went 'boom'!"

Professor Grewal smiled at Noah and then looked back at me and Mr. Withers. "Aniyah?" she asked.

I thought about what to say. I knew Professor Grewal and Mr. Withers and maybe lots of the other people in the room staring at me were star hunters, or at least knew more about stars than normal people did. And I was sure that all of them knew about how stars are born and the kinds of noises they make. But what if they had never heard a real heart being turned into a star like me and Noah had? What if they had only ever read about it in libraries but didn't know how horrible and deafening it was? Just reading about things couldn't ever be the same as hearing or seeing or feeling the thing in real life. But I had to try to make them understand. Mum's star needed me to. And Miss Audrey was the biggest star in Hollywood, which meant she might know all about stars and could help me make everyone understand too.

"Because I heard her," I said simply. "When the policeman and the woman in the black suit came and started talking. I heard the explosion and the sound of Mum's heart leaving and I knew she'd find a way of telling us where she was and where to find her. And she did."

"I see . . . ," said Professor Grewal again. Her nose must have been tickling her because she had to rub it a few times. Mr. Withers's nose must have been tickling him too, because he was scrunching it up and down like a gerbil's.

I could see Frank starting to frown. "What was your mum's name?" he asked, his voice much nicer now.

Travis and Ben looked over at me, and Noah stopped hiccuping as he waited to hear it.

I opened my mouth. "Isabella Hildon," I said, loudly and clearly. It was the first time anyone had asked me her name since she had left us and saying it out loud made my chest feel funny. As if something that had been sleeping inside for a long time had woken up and wanted to dance.

"Isabella . . . Hildon . . . ?" asked a man somewhere in the crowd.

"Oh dear!" whispered a woman.

"Oh, poor things!" cried another woman.

"Tragedy," mumbled a man standing over my shoulder.

Someone in a bright green dress leaned forward and whispered something into Professor Grewal's ear, who then whispered it to Miss Audrey.

"Oh!" cried Miss Audrey as she covered her mouth with both her hands. Frank shook his head and looked at us sadly, and Ben and Travis looked at each other and then at my knees.

Tapping Frank on his shoulder, Mr. Withers cupped his hands around his mouth and said something that made Frank nod and then quickly leave the room. I saw him getting out a walkie-talkie and knew right away what was going to happen!

"Please!" I cried out, trying to stand up. "Please don't call the police! We didn't—we didn't do anything wrong!"

"Calm down, honey," said Miss Audrey, patting my arm and pulling me back down onto the chair. "You're not in trouble, OK? Not at all!"

"We're not?" asked Ben, looking as if he wasn't sure he could trust the best actress in the world.

Miss Audrey shook her head and smiled at him, making Ben look at the floor so hard that I was sure he was going to lean over and fall down.

"We're letting everyone know you're safe," said Professor Grewal. "A lot of people have been very worried about you."

"They—they have?" asked Travis.

Mr. Withers and Professor Grewal nodded.

"Of course," said Professor Grewal. "They just need to know you're safe. They'll be so glad to hear you're here and not trying to find Aniyah's dad."

"My dad?" I asked, wondering why I would be trying to find Dad when it was him who had to try to find us. That's what Mum had said when she had taken us away from school and made us run away to the hotel-that-

255

wasn't-really-a-hotel. That we were the hiders and he was the seeker, and that we had to play the longest game of hide-and-seek that anyone had ever played.

"Oh. Professor Grewal. I don't think we should say anything else," said Miss Audrey, holding my hand.

"I'll go have a word with the Kronos team," said Mr. Withers, clearing his throat. "You know . . . see what we can do."

I saw Professor Grewal nod and Miss Audrey say something, but I couldn't understand her words. My heart was pounding so hard that I didn't know if it was still in my chest or if it had moved to somewhere inside my head. There was something wrong. Why did everyone think I was looking for Dad? In a flash, the voice of the woman in the black suit echoed around my head. She had said something in the car that day—the day she had taken me and Noah away from the hotel-that-wasn't-really-a-hotel. If only I could remember! She had said . . . she had said that we were going to be safe now. That we couldn't be hurt anymore because Dad . . . *Dad* wouldn't be able to find us. . . .

And then suddenly, like a rush of giant waves trying to drown me, I remembered the news flash and the words *murder suspect* and the police officers taking off their hats and telling us Mum had been taken and Katie crying so much at the hotel-that-wasn't-really-a-hotel that she had made both my shoulders wet. And I remembered not just one noise, but all the noises. How there had been a crack from inside that had made my heart split into two—and another crack from high up in the sky. And I knew. I knew Mum's heart hadn't left us because it had wanted to! It had been stolen. Father Time had finally stopped playing his tricks on me and was giving me back all the things I couldn't remember!

But now I didn't want to remember. Not anymore. Not when it meant knowing that Mum's life had been taken by a thief. And that the thief had been my dad.

23

The Seven Sisters

"Niyah . . . don't cry," said Noah as, crying himself, he crawled up onto my knees and tried to wipe away my tears. I could hear sniffles echoing all around the room and people whispering for tissues, as if everyone around us had had their hearts broken too. I didn't want to cry in front of them. I wanted to be on my own and go to sleep and never, ever wake up again. But I couldn't stop crying and I couldn't stop my face from feeling as if it was burning again.

Miss Audrey was wiping away a tear and everyone around us had fallen silent. I could see Ben and Travis wiping their faces too, and wondered if they had known. I wanted to know if Mrs. Iwuchukwu knew—and Sophie too. And why they had never said anything to me if they had.

"Aniyah," said Professor Grewal quietly. "How about we go take a look at your mum's star now? You probably already know this, since you're a star hunter, but we have one of the biggest, most wonderful telescopes in the world a few doors away from us."

I looked up, feeling hopeful. "Really?" I asked, wiping my face dry with my tiger sleeves. "Can Noah and Ben and Travis come too?"

Professor Grewal smiled. "Of course! Audrey, would you like to join us?"

Miss Audrey smiled and stood with a rustle that made her black dress rise like a flower turning back into a bud, holding out her hand to me.

Jumping to their feet, Travis and Ben joined me and Noah, and we all followed Professor Grewal and Miss Audrey and Mr. Withers out of the room. As the crowd of penguin-suited men and shimmering ladies stood aside to let us pass, I felt hands patting me on the back and people whispering, "Brave girl!"

Reaching a small door behind the stage, Mr. Withers got out a card, beeped it next to a machine, and held the door open for us. Behind it was a tiny corridor. Professor Grewal and Miss Audrey stayed by my side as we walked through lots of corridors, until we reached a large steel door that looked as if it belonged to a bank. Above it, in

large golden letters, was a sign that said THE GREAT EQUATO-
RIAL TELESCOPE, 1893.

"Here we are." Professor Grewal smiled as Mr. Withers grabbed the handle and, with a loud thud, pushed the
door open, which made the lights flicker on.

"After you, Aniyah," whispered Professor Grewal,
pointing to the room with her head.

I took a step onto the red-and-black-tiled floor that
looked like a never-ending chessboard, and gazed up.
There in front of me was the longest, shiniest white telescope I had ever seen, stretching like a brand-new road
leading straight into the sky. All around it were lines of
white metal that crissed and crossed across the ceiling like
a giant web, right up to the huge pointy dome above the
telescope.

Taking out a special red-colored key from her pocket,
Professor Grewal went up to a metal box high up on the
wall and, swinging it open, slotted the key into a hole near
a large yellow button.

"Flying pancakes . . . ," whispered Ben as Noah grabbed
my hand and Travis's mouth fell open.

Together we stood and watched as, from high above,
the web started to move and the dome began to split apart,
like a giant eyelid that was beginning to open.

After Professor Grewal had made the eye open all the

way, she sat down in a special chair, and began to turn lots of wheels and knobs and spinning dials to make the telescope turn and tilt and help her search for my mum's star.

"Will this help?" I asked, suddenly remembering the star map I had made.

Professor Grewal opened up the now very scrunchy piece of paper, and held it to the light so that she could see it better.

"This is very good," she said, and Miss Audrey took it and looked too. "Where did you draw that?" she asked, looking at me with a smile.

"From my window at Mrs. Iwuchukwu's," I said. "The one at the back of the house—not the front."

"Mrs. Iwuchukwu?" asked Professor Grewal.

"Our f-foshter mum," explained Travis, taking a step forward and then a step back again, as if he was speaking to a general.

"Ah," said Professor Grewal.

She walked over to Mr. Withers and spoke to him in whispers as he busily typed things into a large computer. Above us, the giant telescope moved to the left and then down and then up and down again, until Mr. Withers finally went, "Aha!"

"That's it," said Professor Grewal. "Come and have a look, Aniyah."

Professor Grewal lifted me onto the seat so I could see better. She helped me put my eye to the telescope. For a few seconds, everything went black, and then I saw her. A fiery bluish-white ball of light.

Pushing my eye further into the eyepiece, I whispered, "Hello, Mum!" The star seemed to shine brighter for a second, as if it had heard me.

"I want to see Mum!" whispered Noah, pulling on my tail. Professor Grewal helped him up onto my lap and showed him too. After he kept asking, "Where? Where?" he finally seemed to see Mum, and gave her a wave and blew her a loud kiss.

"Where is she going?" I asked, remembering how the news report had said she was traveling across the sky, and wondering if Mum had defied the laws of physics because she was trying to get to somewhere special.

"Let's see, shall we?" said Mr. Withers as he moved the telescope a few millimeters to the side with some dials. Checking to see it was where he wanted it to be, he told me to look again.

"Can you see a shape made up of some extra-bright blue stars there?" he asked. "Like Orion's Belt but longer and made up of four big stars instead of three—sort of like a wonky tail?"

I nodded, because the telescope was so big and powerful I could see the shape without even having to imagine it!

"And below those four bright stars, can you see another three floating underneath them, like a hook?"

I nodded again as I tried not to blink. I didn't ever want to forget what I was seeing.

"Well, those seven stars form a special cluster called the Pleiades constellation—or the Seven Sisters," explained Mr. Withers. "They're the brightest, most famous sisters in all the universe, because they lie closest to the earth. Ever since the beginning of time, they have always been there, looking down on us. It's thought that each of those stars are more than a hundred times brighter than our sun."

"Really?" I asked.

"Whoa! No way!" cried Ben.

"Why are they called the S-Seven Sistersh?" asked Travis, edging closer toward the telescope.

"Maybe Miss Audrey can tell you that?" Professor Grewal smiled.

"Well, I do actually know this one, since I played one of them in a movie," said Miss Audrey as she gave Noah's hair a stroke and squeezed my shoulder. "You see, legend has it that the seven sisters were once the most beautiful women on earth, and they loved to do nothing better than dance under the night sky. But one day, a hunter called Orion wanted to take them, and so he chased them and chased them and chased them. He chased them for seven whole years, which of course made the sisters incredibly afraid and tired. So Zeus, the god of the skies and thunder, decided to hide them away for good and make sure Orion could never reach them, by turning them all into stars!"

"Whoa!" said Ben again.

"And he didn't stop there," Miss Audrey said with a smile. "He turned Orion into a constellation too, and placed him on the other side of the sky so that he could never, ever reach the seven sisters again, and so that they would be safe forever!"

"G-good!" said Travis angrily.

"Now, the reason why we're showing them to Aniyah," said Professor Grewal, "is—"

Professor Grewal stopped talking, as from a distance we could hear loud cries and footsteps and shouting.

Ben and Travis looked at me, their eyes wide with fear and surprise.

"There you are!" cried a voice as the door to the Equatorial Room flew open.

"*Mum!*" shouted Ben and Travis as Mrs. Iwuchukwu ran in and, diving toward us, began crying and hugging and touching our faces. Sophie walked in behind her, but she looked red and embarrassed and kept looking over her shoulder at Frank and the two police officers who were holding their helmets in their hands.

I watched as Ben said sorry and Travis nodded and Noah looked scared but happy and Miss Audrey shook hands with everyone, but I couldn't move or talk or say anything. I felt as if I was frozen in time, and could only watch everyone else moving and feeling things apart from me.

"How did you get here so quick?" asked Ben, hugging Mrs. Iwuchukwu so hard she had to loosen his arms and tell him to let her breathe.

"We were with the police in London already!" cried Mrs. Iwuchukwu, her whole face so wet and shiny it looked like a brand-new ice rink. "As soon as we heard you were at Victoria Station this morning we came down, but the police lost you! Then a woman said she had seen you all going into the Greenwich Foot Tunnel, but we were too late again!"

"Oh! The ice cream w-woman!" said Travis happily.

"Good thing too, otherwise I think I would have gone mad," said Mrs. Iwuchukwu, shaking her head. Then, turning to me, she asked, "Now, what's all this about a star?"

Everyone looked at me, but I kept looking at the floor. Something red and fiery was starting to grow inside me, and I had to let it out. It was hurting me too much.

Looking up at Mrs. Iwuchukwu, I asked her, "Did you know . . . about my dad? And what he did?"

I heard Miss Audrey sniff and saw Noah staring at me looking confused and Ben and Travis looking worried.

Mrs. Iwuchukwu didn't say anything but came and took my hands.

"Yes, Aniyah, I knew. Because it's my job to know. And to protect you."

I watched as Mrs. Iwuchukwu's glittery eyes filled with tears, and as Miss Audrey's did the same.

"Mrs. I. made us promise not to tell," said Ben quietly as he came to stand in front of me too. "But it's because we're not supposed to talk to you about stuff that might hurt you, and we didn't want to say anything wrong. Not because we were trying to keep secrets or anything."

Travis nodded quickly and looked at me through his fringe.

Red-hot stinging drops of water began to burn my eyes again and fall down my cheeks. It felt as if everyone had lied to me.

"I know it will have been hard for you to remember everything, darling," said Mrs. Iwuchukwu as she gripped my hands tighter and tighter. "And I know how confusing it can be and how unfair it all is. But we're all here to help you, eh?"

Everyone nodded at me as Noah clung on to my arm, his face making it wet.

"Oh, Aniyah! We're so sorry!" said Professor Grewal. Her face was wet too and her eye makeup was beginning to fall down her face, which made her start to look like a panda bear.

I nodded back and tried to dry my eyes, but they wouldn't stop leaking. I opened my mouth to tell everyone that it was OK, because Mum's heart was so strong that she hadn't lost us and was never going to leave us and that I was lucky because I had seen her heart burning in the sky too. But instead of making words, my body made a long and wailing cry.

Pulling me toward her, Mrs. Iwuchukwu squeezed me into a hug and didn't let me push her away, while Miss Audrey hugged me from the back.

"None of it is your fault, Aniyah," whispered Mrs. Iwuchukwu as she stroked my hair and gave a long, sad sigh. "Your mum loved you, and you loved your mum, and that's all that matters."

I opened my mouth again because I wanted to say that it wasn't all that mattered. Because I hadn't saved her.

Nobody had saved her! But instead, my throat made another wailing sound and then fell quiet.

After what felt like a very long time, I felt the burning in my eyes begin to disappear, and someone's hands come and hold some of my fingers that were squeezed under Mrs. Iwuchukwu's arms. At first I thought it was Noah, because no one but Mum and Noah ever held my fingers, but when I looked down, I saw that the hand was white and freckly.

I looked up over Mrs. Iwuchukwu's shoulder, feeling surprised. Sophie was standing in front of me, her eyes wet and red too.

"Here," she said, holding out my locket. "I'm sorry I took it from you."

I pushed away from Mrs. Iwuchukwu and looked down at the locket in my hand. It felt strange to have it back now that I knew Dad was a thief. Somehow it felt different. I knew I couldn't ever wear it again, but I also knew that I wanted to keep it, because of Mum.

Just then, Frank came back into the room. Holding the door open behind him, he announced, "We're all ready, everybody. Time to go."

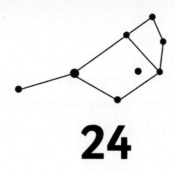

24

The Star Outside My Window

"Are we really ready?" asked Professor Grewal, her panda eyes now even worse than they were before.

Frank nodded. "Everything's set up. Miss Audrey just has to lead the way!"

Professor Grewal helped me down from the telescope seat and gave me a hug that was so tight it made me hold my breath. "Aniyah, I think you're a very special girl, and that your mum must have been extra special to have left the world someone like you."

I nodded, but only because I knew Mum was extra special. Not because I was.

"And because she was so special, and you're so special, and Noah is so special . . ." Professor Grewal looked at Noah and gave his face a stroke. "Well, come on . . . you'll see!"

Miss Audrey held her arm out to me. I grabbed it with one arm as Professor Grewal took Noah's, and Ben and Travis and Sophie and Mrs. Iwuchukwu and Mr. Withers followed us out.

"Easy does it," said Frank, holding open the metal doors for us and giving me a wink.

As Travis and Ben and Professor Grewal all tried to help me hop alongside them, we made our way back down the corridors and into the big room with the stage and the cinema screen and the tables filled with people wearing diamonds and penguin suits. As soon as the doors opened, a million cameras clicked and flashed and whizzed and popped. Somewhere in the distance, people began to clap and shout, "Bravo!" as Professor Grewal and Mr. Withers placed all of us into some chairs right at the front of the room.

"Here we go!" whispered Miss Audrey as she stepped up onto the stage. Everyone gave a loud cheer before gradually falling quiet.

"Ladies and gentlemen," said Miss Audrey. "Thank you for your patience. And to those watching on our live feed, thank you for your patience too!"

Stopping to wave at the largest camera in the room, Miss Audrey gave it a wink too.

"Tonight, under circumstances almost as unique, as

special, and as wondrous as the phenomenon now traveling across our galaxy, I am pleased to unveil to you the name of our new star!"

The screen behind the stage, which had been black, began to flash the words *Kronos Enterprise and the Royal Observatory Greenwich Are Proud to Present . . .*

"Drumroll, please!" shouted Miss Audrey, and the sound of drums began again. "And now, in memory of a very special mother, and for her two young starlings here with us today, the Kronos Enterprise and the Royal Observatory Board have agreed to name the new star . . ." Miss Audrey swept to the side of the stage and pointed to the large screen behind her. Eight letters flashed up in the most sparkling golden writing I had ever seen, spelling out the word:

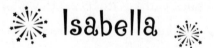

The room behind us burst into applause. Ben and Travis jumped up from their chairs and begin to whoop and punch the air while Sophie hugged Noah and Noah pushed her away, and Professor Grewal held Mrs. Iwuchukwu's hand so tight that it began to turn white.

"But! That's not all!" said Miss Audrey as she used her hands like an orchestra leader to make everyone quiet again. "Thanks to our 'star hunters' here at the observatory, we can now bring you a live feed of Isabella as she travels through our solar system."

The screen with Mum's name on it changed and went black again. But this time, in the middle of the blackness was a small white dot.

Mr. Withers now jumped up on the stage and pointed at the dot. "That there is our star, Isabella," he said into a microphone, looking down at me with a smile. "And if our whiz team can hear me, let's zoom out so we can see which direction she's heading in."

The screen looked like it was whooshing backward, and Mum's star became smaller and smaller and smaller, until she was surrounded by lots of other white dots.

Starting from where Mum's dot had been, Mr. Withers made a straight line with his fingers and, walking across the stage, pointed to what looked like seven dots all squeezed together right in the top corner.

"It seems Isabella is on a straight trajectory toward the Pleiades constellation," explained Mr. Withers, "the constellation of the Seven Sisters and their parents, Atlas and Pleione. Where, we hope, she'll be finding herself in the best of families!"

Everyone in the room began clapping again, and

Professor Grewal gave my knees a squeeze. I stared at the screen and at the small dots of light that Mum was traveling to, feeling so happy that my head hurt. Mum wasn't ever going to be alone! She was going to live with a family that was waiting for her—just like Mrs. Iwuchukwu's family had been waiting for me and Noah. She was heading to a foster family and, just like me, was going to be a foster sister too.

The next day and the next day and the next day after that, Mum's star was in all the papers and on all the television channels. I had to stay in a hospital for two of those days, because the doctors said I had torn something near my ankle that needed to be fixed properly and that meant I couldn't move. But I didn't mind, because Ben and Travis brought me all the newspapers, and Mrs. Iwuchukwu gave me a big book to cut out and stick all the stories in so that I could save them forever.

Professor Grewal and Mr. Withers didn't visit me, but they did send me an extra-special parcel. It was the biggest parcel I had ever been sent, and Mrs. Iwuchukwu saved it for me as a present to open when I got home from the hospital. As soon as I got in through the door and hopped to the living room, Travis and Ben ran and got it and put it on top of the coffee table in front of me.

"Go on!" said Ben as he stopped Noah's hands from opening the package first. "Unless—you want me to do it?"

I shook my head.

"Yeah, Ben! Let her open it!" said Sophie, coming into the room and sitting on the sofa opposite. "It's her leg that got hurt! Not her hands!"

Ben shrugged as everyone leaned in to watch me.

"Hold on! Hold on!" cried out Mrs. Iwuchukwu as she ran in with a camera in her hands. "Right! Now, *go!*" she ordered, standing behind Sophie and holding the camera up. As soon as I began to tear it open with my hands, and then my teeth, Mrs. Iwuchukwu began to click and flash away.

"Whoa!" said Ben as a huge ball of bubble wrap fell out.

"That's jusht the p-packaging!" sighed Travis as he shook his head.

Undoing the bubble wrap, I opened it up to find a small golden envelope and a square black box.

"That's a Kronos box!" cried Ben, pointing at it and then jumping to his feet and grabbing his hair. "It's the watch! It has to be the watch! Aw, man!"

"Aniyah, why don't you start with the card first?"

Mrs. Iwuchukwu smiled. "I'm sure it'll explain everything."

Nodding, I picked up the envelope and took out the small white card inside.

It read:

Dear Aniyah,

Please find enclosed a gift to you from Kronos Watches: a unique, handcrafted watch to commemorate the 250th year of their enterprise. This gift has been enhanced with a design of your mother's name, created and gifted by Miss Audrey Tahania, and sent with her love.

We trust that you will come to visit us soon so we can hear all about your developments in the field of star hunting! And until then, we leave you, Noah, Travis, and Ben with hopes that all your days and nights are filled with light and stardust.

Yours sincerely,
Professor Jasmine Grewal
and Mr. Alex Withers

I put down the card and picked up the black box, feeling both Noah and Ben pushing in on me. As I clicked the box open, we all looked down. Nobody made a sound, or clapped, or gasped, or grabbed it. Because it was too beautiful to make us want to do any of those things. Instead we just stared and stared.

For there was the watch we had seen on the web page for the biggest competition in the galaxy. It had the exact same silver numbers going all the way around it, the same large hand with a silver shooting star on it, the same small hand with a crescent moon, and the same *Kronos 250* written in tiny golden writing in the middle. But instead of random tiny stars shining out from different parts of the navy-blue face, the stars had all been joined up like a constellation to spell the word *Isabella.*

I held the watch in my hands and smiled. Mum's name was going to be on my wrist for all time, and Noah and me had two new brothers and a sister to help us feel like a family again. But best of all, Mum's star had found a new home too, right outside my window, where I could find her whenever I needed to, and from where she could always watch over all of us. So as Mrs. Iwuchukwu raised her camera one more time, I looked straight up into the shiny round lens and smiled my best smile, because I knew I had everything I could ever need to be the luckiest star hunter on earth.

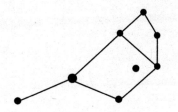

What Is Domestic Abuse?

In this story, Aniyah, Noah, Ben, and Travis have each seen or experienced domestic abuse in different ways.

Domestic abuse is the act of one person trying to hurt, control, and frighten another. There are many ways an abuser (the person causing the hurt) can hurt someone. They may use physical violence, but they may also use words to cause hurt or fear, or purposefully make someone feel confused, stupid, and less confident. Many abusers often also try to control their victim(s) by cutting them off from friends and family or restricting their access to money.

The act of hurting or trying to control another human being is against the law, and is not something anyone of any age should have to live with.

Some Facts and Questions
for Human Computers
to Explore . . .

Aniyah's story may have prompted lots of questions. If you would like to learn more about the real-life issues that inspired this story, you can ask a parent, teacher, or other trusted adult to visit makingherstory.org.uk with you, where you will find some facts and questions to discuss.

The Stars in This Story

At the beginning of each chapter in this story (and at the end of the very last one!), there is a drawing of a constellation. Constellations are very special, because as Aniyah said, they tell a story.

Here are the names of the constellation from each chapter. We hope you enjoy finding out their stories—and how they tie in with Aniyah's adventures.

Chapter 1	Leo & Leo Minor
Chapter 2	Lyra
Chapter 3	Cygnus
Chapter 4	Taurus
Chapter 5	Sagitta
Chapter 6	Horologium
Chapter 7	Lepus
Chapter 8	Auriga
Chapter 9	Hydra
Chapter 10	Scorpio
Chapter 11	Caelum

Author's Note

Ever since I can remember, I have always been aware of just how unfair life can be for girls—girls destined to be women. It impacted my childhood so much that I was constantly told off for asking "too many questions." Questions like: Why weren't there ever any female Teenage Mutant Ninja Turtles? Why was there a motion picture for He-Man but never one for She-Ra? Why was I called a tomboy for preferring jeans and basketball to Barbie dolls and kiss-chase—why couldn't I just be me? And why was I always teased for being a teacher's pet at school for wanting the best grades, but no equally ambitious boy ever was?

As I grew older, my ponderings became questions that frustrated me. And later, both at university and in my working life, I was constantly rocked to my core on learning of the universality of women's struggles for the basic right to be treated humanely and with as much dignity and respect as men.

But for all my studies, awareness, and questions, I was not prepared for the way my world would shatter on July 5, 2011, when a dear member of my family—someone we had tried so desperately to free from a dangerous, violent man—was taken from us. My aunt, Mumtahina "Ruma" Jannat, fought for five whole years to save her own life, using every limited means she had to prove to anyone who would listen that she was in danger. But no one—not even the judges overseeing her case—believed her.

In 2012, I officially launched Making Herstory in her memory. Making Herstory has one simple core aim: to mobilize whoever we can to tackle violence against women and girls in all its forms. I never imagined I would write a children's book centered on the experiences of some of the brave women and children I have met in countless women's shelters, or indeed on my aunt's experience. But here it is . . . along with the hope that maybe, somehow, it will help someone break free.

If You Are a Little Survivor . . .

If, like Aniyah, Noah, Ben, or Travis, you have been hurt or are scared by the actions of a grown-up in your world—whether that is at home or elsewhere—there are lots of wonderful people waiting to help you.

The most important thing to remember is that you are not alone, and that the first step to getting help for yourself and your loved ones is telling someone.

That can be especially hard to do when the person causing you fear or pain is someone you know, but it is crucial. You may want to tell a teacher or your doctor, but **if you feel you can't speak to anyone that you know, you can contact the help line that appears below.** And always remember that if you ever find yourself in immediate danger, call 911, or ask someone near you to call 911.

If You Are Not-So-Little . . .

If you are an adult survivor, or know of someone who is, you may like to access help for yourself or a loved one you can **contact the help line that appears below**.

National Domestic Violence Hotline
1-800-799-SAFE (7233)

Acknowledgments

This story, from its conception to becoming a real and actual book, has constituted one of the most difficult tasks of my life. I would not have survived the journey without the following people, and while I'm not sure if words can ever do them justice, I can try. . . .

To my eternal rocks, Mum and Zak: thank you for bearing with me through my "Gollum" days whilst I battled with this story. Somehow you kept me watered and fed through my struggles across my inner Mordor, and led me back out into the Shire (this metaphor would be hilarious if weren't so painfully true—and my feet weren't quite so hairy!). I will never be able to thank you enough. And, Zak, I owe you times infinity for reminding me about those precious words Mufasa said to Simba in *The Lion King*. Finally, our childhood obsession with Disney cartoons has paid off!

To my knight in literary armor and an agent that could give James Bond a run for his martinis, Silvia Molteni: I still don't have the words to express how huge a part you continue to play in revolutionizing my life. I am in awe at it all, and only hope that one day, you'll get to see for yourself the impact your faith in me has had—not just on me, but also on the worlds that make up my own one. Thank you for understanding me, taking care of me, and guiding me through the maze of this past year. I'd literally be lost without you.

This book would in no way, shape, form, or thought have come to exist without one person. Lena McCauley: an editor who outdoes all other editors. That have ever existed. Ever. Like the perfect partner in any birthing room, you have held my hands, breathed, nodded, encouraged, stepped back, whispered, and steered me through what turned out to be an incredibly difficult being to bring into the world. I don't think I will ever truly believe this is real and has finally led to a second book forged of real live atoms. You are this book's other parent, and both it and I know that as it takes its first steps out into the world, we couldn't have asked for anyone better. Thank you from the very bottom of my heart to the tip of every star in my sky for your incredible calm and patience, and for giving me all the space I needed to get this story out of me. It's here! We did it! Really!

Pippa Curnick: I honestly believe you are the wielder of a magic brush. Thank you for another gorgeous cover for and expanding the internal world of the story with your vision and creativity. Nothing you have ever gifted me is less than stunning. And Emma Roberts, Alison Padley, and Sophie—I am so grateful to you all for stepping in to tighten up the story and make it shipshape and ready for launching with your eagle-eyed proofing, design, and editing skills.

To my chief maestro, Dominic Kingston: thank you for all your hard work, your dedication, and your eternal capacity to make PR-ing seem so easy. You and my Hachette PR family—Becci Mansell, Emily Thomas, Fiona Evans, and Lucy Clayton (and now James McParland)—have been so stupendous in supporting me through the whirlwind that has been becoming a Real Author that I feel thoroughly blessed. I owe you all—together with Helen Thomas and Ruth Alltimes—a lifetime of teas and at least three thousand carousel rides for being my stabilizers.

To Anoushka Khan, dear friend and a clinical psychologist who gives her all to helping little ones deal with every un/imaginable cruelty life can throw at them: I want to thank you for your calm advice and beautiful help in ensuring I understood the confusions, heartaches, and frustrating procedures involved for children who have to live with the unthinkable. I am more grateful than you can ever know for introducing me to David Trickey and Katherine Mautner at the Anna Freud Centre, who in turn have their place in this story for the kindness, time, and expertise they gifted me. Long may you all go on in your crucial works with children who deserve so much more of the world's love and support.

To the passionate volunteers, guides, and astronomers at the Royal Observatory Greenwich: thank you for bearing with my questions—no matter how worrying they may have sounded (breaking in, squirrels, and stars crashing through hemispheres notwithstanding)! My especial thanks to Megan Soley for squeezing me in to sold-out stargazing shows; Greg the Volunteer, who let me push the button to rotate the Great Equatorial Telescope—it was a highlight of my life; and Kirsty Schaper, Sheryl Twigg, Brendan Owens, Elizabeth Bowers, and James Gill for acting so quickly to ensure we got it all right.

To the amazing souls who have supported Making Herstory's (MH) dreams of eradicating all forms of violence against women and girls: you light up my world. Remona Aly (the beat to my heart); Micky and Sandy Youngson (setting the world straight together); Lusa Nsenga Ngoy (the calm amid the storm); Doreen Samuels (a true champion of hearts); Elisabeth Grellet (you cycled from London to Paris for MH—I will never forget it); Yasmin Ishaq (queen mobilizer and warrior to the core); Jude Habib (thank you for helping me confront my stories); Alexandra Barker (bridge builder along with the Paul Hamlyn Foundation);

Karen Ingala-Smith and the NIA (your life-saving works inspire me: please keep counting); Satdeep Grewal and Alex Thomas (aka Professor Grewal and Alex Withers!—thank you for being my Flowers of Hope) together with Rabia Barkatulla (you are all everlasting MH guardians); Nadia Abouayoub (for being there from the beginning); Selma Avci and Turgay Ozcan (soul mates in every fight!); Asha Abdillahi (beloved cheerer); Sughra Ahmed (my touchstone!); Piya Muqit (a warrior until the end); Shaista Chisty (mind blower); Ayisha Malik (Authoress Supreme and Lifelong Inspiration); Sumiya Hemsi (fierce defender for so many survivors); Julie Siddiqi (FFFL—Fellow Feminist For Life); Homaira Sofia Khan and Atif Butt (my go-to healers); Rose Sanders (most loyal Herstory Maker); John Crawford and Victoria Dyke (my fairy godparents); Kamilah, Eshan, Zahir, Inara, and Rayan (my heart's healers); and every Herstory Maker who has stepped up to help the women and girls of our worlds—I quite literally wouldn't be here if it weren't for every single one of you.

I cannot draw this book to a close without writing out the name of one whose life—and death—changed my world irrevocably. That name being Mumtahina "Ruma" Jannat. There are three things the world needs to know about my aunt Ruma: she made the most delicious caramel egg pudding you could ever hope to taste. She rarely laughed, but when she did, it made your heart laugh too. And she loved her two gorgeous little daughters more than anything else in this universe. All facts which still make it unbearable for me to accept that her life was stolen from us by a man who couldn't bear that she should be free of him. She was just twenty-nine at the time. It is with my aunt and the injustices she faced in her lifetime in mind that this book was written. I can only hope that, were she alive, my aunt would smile, nod, and give me a hug of approval at its creation.

To all women and children currently living with domestic abuse, please know you are not alone, and that there are amazing people out there who are fighting with every ounce of strength they have to change the unjust laws and systems currently governing our world. I hope you find the road to safety and freedom one day, and that we can all—both men and women—be freed from all forms of toxic violence.

To every foster or adoptive parent, stepping in to help children come to terms with a chaos they had no hand in creating: you are truly amazing. In particular, my love and deepest thanks to my now-adopted aunt and uncle, Sabia Begum and Afsorul Islam—the couple who stepped in, fought for, and came to love my nieces as their own daughters while my own family fell apart. You were the foster parents of our dreams and healed our worlds. Thank you for loving Maeesha and Kasheefa with your whole hearts.

To every foster child looking for love and a place to call home: I hope you find both in abundance soon, and come to meet those who will love you for all that you are. No matter how tall you become.

And last but never least, the deepest wells of gratitude in my heart go out to God: for every moment S/He continues to gift me, and every story brought my way.

About the Author

Onjali Q. Raúf is the founder of Making Herstory, an organization that encourages men, women, and children to work together to create a fairer and more equal world for women and girls everywhere. Her first novel, *The Boy at the Back of the Class,* won the Blue Peter Book Award as well as the Waterstones Children's Book Prize. Her most recent novel is *The Night Bus Hero.*

 @OnjaliRauf

Don't miss . . .

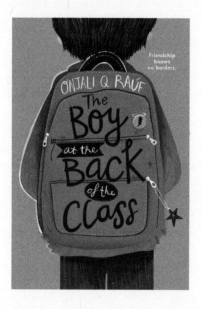

Balancing humor and heart, this relatable novel explores the refugee crisis from the perspective of kids and reminds readers that everyone deserves a place to call home.

★ "This moving and timely debut novel tells an enlightening, empowering, and ultimately hopeful story about how compassion and a willingness to speak out can change the world."
—*School Library Journal*

Winner of the Waterstones Children's Book Prize
Winner of the Blue Peter Book Award